Women of
The Ring

SALLY J. LING

Flamingo
Press

ACKNOWLEDGEMENTS

My sincere thanks to editor, Susan Bryant, and the select individuals who assisted in the reading of *Women of the Ring*.

All photos are public domain with the exception of Mosie Boulay. See below for image credits.

Mary (Mary of Burgundy) – Michael Pacher, c. 1490
Catherine de' Medici – Francois Clouet, c. 1555
Scullery Maid – Jean Baptiste-Siméon Chardin, c. 1738
Mosie Boulay – Reprinted by permission of Laila Duran, Duran Textiles
Grace Elliott – Thomas Gainsborough, c. 1778
Georgina Cavendish-Bentinck – c. prior to 1883
Sarah Bernhardt – Felix Nadar, c. 1864

Women of
The Ring

Chapter 1

It began as an ordinary day. It didn't end that way.

Abel Moody's narrow shoulders hunched over his worn wooden desk in the back of his one-man jewelry shop in Brooklyn, New York. Behind him, an organized workbench lined the wall. Tools hung from a pegboard above it, bordered by small drawers reminiscent of an old apothecary shop. These were stuffed with soldering irons, silver and gold wire, prongs of various sizes and configurations, tins of flux and the like. Loose diamonds, faceted gem stones, and important documents were kept in a large steel safe that ran the width of the wall at the end of the worktable.

Wearing a leather apron and jeweler's magnifying glasses, Abel meticulously examined each gem in the exquisite necklace he grasped in his long, calloused fingers. A wealthy customer had commissioned the band of diamonds interspersed with rubies as a fortieth anniversary gift to his wife. As Abel was documenting the clarity, cut, and carat size of the main gem for insurance purposes, the electronic bell at his front door sounded.

He slid the magnifying glasses onto his head and glanced through the doorway of his compact workspace past the jewelry cases to the locked front door. Through it, he saw a young woman with a pale, oval face, her brunette hair bound in a scarlet red shawl. The rest of her was bundled in a black wool coat against the stinging January wind that fluttered scraps of debris and newspapers down the street behind her. She waved a gloved hand in greeting.

Abel pressed the buzzer hidden under his desk, and the bolt on the door recoiled with a thud. He slid the diamond necklace into a black velvet box, locked it in his top drawer, and fixed his wire-rimmed glasses on his wide nose. Grabbing his cane, support for his arthritic hip, he ambled to the counter as the woman entered the store.

"Oh, Miss Julia, hard to see who you were all bundled up. It's so good to see you. It's been a long time." White dentures gleamed behind Abel's broad smile as he slipped around the counter to give a warm hug to the woman with rosy cheeks and sparkling green eyes, her bangs almost covering them.

"I can't believe it's been what . . . three years since I've seen you?" Julia returned the hug just as warmly but remembered the jeweler as far more robust. Her arms wrapped around a thin frame that seemed frail now. She removed her shawl and gloves and laid them on the counter with her Coach Edie shoulder bag.

"Time sure does fly. I guess we've both been busy," said Abel, trying to be understanding.

"It's work, Mr. Moody. Trying to keep customers walking in the latest fashion is very demanding."

"Not too demanding, though, I see you're getting married. It seems like only yesterday you were a young girl looking wide-eyed at the sparkling jewels in my window." Abel's brows spiked above his dark eyes as he peeped at Julia over the rim of his glasses.

Julia let out a muffled laugh. "I'm thirty-two now, Mr. Moody. Don't you think it's time?"

Abel threw up his hands. "Thirty-two! Girls are sure waiting longer these days. In my day, they married in their late teens and had children by twenty. But times have changed."

"Thank goodness," Julia said with a smile.

"Well, how can I help you, Miss Julia?"

"Before I tell you that, I hear through the grapevine that you're retiring soon. I simply can't imagine this Brooklyn neighborhood without you."

Abel let out a deep sigh and scanned his shop as though bygone memories were etched in every mirror, clock, or light fixture on the walls or piece of glittering jewelry.

"I'm getting older, Miss Julia. Seventy-eight this year. Edna, God rest her soul, is gone ten years now. I have no heirs to carry on the Moody name or the family's generations of jewelry crafting. When I retire, the shop will too."

Julia patted Abel's black hand as her eyes welled with tears. "We'll miss the store and you behind the counter, Mr. Moody, but you'll stay in the neighborhood, won't you?"

"Can't get rid of me that easily," he said with a laugh. "Besides, I have no place else to go. I still live above the shop, you know, so I'll stay."

"Good. That makes me feel better."

"So, how can I help you today?" Abel asked.

"Oh, here," Julia said. She withdrew a small white cardboard box from her bag and placed it on the counter.

"My grandmother gave me the ring in this box many years ago. She wanted me to use it for my engagement whenever that day came. It's been in our family for over sixty years, but no one has any idea what it's worth. Winston and I thought we should have it cleaned and insured before the big day. That reminds me, you did get your invitation to the engagement party, didn't you?"

"Of course, Miss Julia. Wouldn't miss that. By the way, this Winston fellow must be very special."

"He is," said Julia, a twinkle in her eye.

"Well, I hope he knows just how special you are." Abel peered at Julia with father-like affection before turning to the box. He was about to open it when a shrill train whistle startled him.

"It's my cell phone," Julia said in apology. "A text message." She pulled an iPhone from the outside pocket of her bag and read the message. "Mr. Moody, I'm so sorry. I'd hoped we'd have more time together, but I've been called back to the office. Here's my business card. Please call me when the ring is ready. We won't officially be engaged until the party, and that isn't for three weeks. I can pick up the ring any time before that. Perhaps we can catch up then over coffee."

"I'd like that," said Abel, slipping Julia's card into his apron pocket.

Julia gave Abel a parting hug and rushed out the door amid a whirlwind of flying scarfs and gloves.

Back at his work desk, Abel removed a small rectangular piece of cotton from inside the box. As he lifted the ring, he let out a loud gasp. Hurriedly, he repositioned his jeweler's glasses for a closer examination.

Adrenaline surged through him, and his heart pounded. His fingers trembled as he exchanged his jeweler's glasses for bifocals. He pulled Julia's card from his pocket

8

and set it on the desk. He recognized the familiar red star of Macy's department store but was unfamiliar with her new position: assistant director of purchasing, women's shoes. His hands shook as he picked up the phone and punched in her cell number.

"Mr. Moody, I didn't expect to hear from you so soon. Don't tell me you've already cleaned and appraised the ring."

"No, no Miss Julia, it's not that." Abel's voice shook.

"Then what, Mr. Moody? Are you all right?" Deep concern permeated Julia's voice.

"I'm fine, I just wanted to know more about the ring." He could hear horns honking in the background and surmised Julia was still on her way back to work.

"Well, like I told you, it belongs to my grandmother Frances."

"Other than that, do you know any of its history?"

"From what I understand, it was given to her by Vera, my great-great aunt. Vera actually took it off her finger on her deathbed and pressed it into grandmother's hand. Vera had no children and wanted the ring to remain in the family."

"Do you know how it came into Vera's possession?"

Julia paused. "Mr. Moody, why all the questions?"

"It's just that . . . well, it's such a lovely piece, I wondered what history it might have. I enjoy knowing about the jewelry I work on, especially the older pieces. It's kind of a hobby."

"I see. Well, the ring came to Vera from her sister Louise Lazzari's estate. Louise lived in Boca Raton, Florida, with her husband, Leno. Unfortunately, they were both murdered early one Sunday morning back in 1948."

"How very sad."

"Yes, it was a terrible tragedy," Julia said. "What made it worse is that their murders were never solved. To this day, it's still a cold case."

"If it's not too much trouble, Miss Julia, do you know how Louise obtained the ring?"

"I was told Louise's employer gave it to her. I heard there was more to the story of the ring, but Louise died before she told anyone just what that was."

"So you don't know where Louise's employer got the ring?"

"No, my understanding is she was a rich Palm Beach socialite who traveled the globe. Maybe she got it somewhere in Europe."

"Do you think your grandmother might know more about the ring's history?"

"She might, Mr. Moody, but she has dementia and doesn't even remember my name. I'm sorry."

"No, no, my dear, it is I who am sorry. Your grandmother is a dear woman who was a loyal customer. I'm saddened to know she isn't well. I'll be in touch when the ring's ready."

After hanging up, Abel sat at his desk contemplating what Julia had told him about the ring's recent history. With reluctance, he glanced down at the lower right drawer of his desk that he hadn't opened in decades. His trembling fingers pulled on the handle. The drawer wouldn't budge. He gave it a couple of strong yanks with both hands. Finally, the drawer yielded to reveal a stack of old papers. Behind it was a little wooden box. Abel placed it on his desk and stared at it. Hesitating. Wondering.

He took a deep breath and lifted the lid. Inside was a key, which he removed before walking to the safe. On a shelf behind his tax records, he located a small locked tin his father had given him before he died. The box had been in his family for more than two centuries, passed on to his father by his grandfather and down to his grandfather from Abel's great-grandfather, each an accomplished jeweler.

He cradled the container as though it were a fragile piece of crystal before unlocking it on his desk. Inside were two folded pieces of paper. His father had been fairly tightlipped about them, until he was on his deathbed. Then he gave Abel a stern warning: "Don't open them unless you plan to do something about them." Abel's father went on in gasps to tell him in no uncertain terms just what that "something" was.

Abel froze in his chair wide-eyed, stunned. As he looked at the papers, opposing emotions swirled in his head: joy, sadness, apprehension, determination. One question pounded through, though, like the thumping of a rap song reverberating from a car window: Should I dare open them?

Yes, he must.

His hands quivered as he lifted the first note from the box and opened it. Appearing less aged than the one underneath, written on it was a man's name, address, and phone number. He tenderly lifted out the second discolored paper and smoothed it out as best he could in its nearly crumbling state. His eyes darted back and forth from a sketch on the paper to Julia's ring, comparing the two in minute detail. Yes, indeed, they were the same.

Abel returned the ring to its cardboard box and slid it into his pocket. He refolded the papers and tucked them into his wallet behind the thin leather flap in the back of the bills section.

Scribbling a hasty note, he taped it to the inside of the front door and turned over the sign to read CLOSED. Next, he switched off the lights and depressed the button to bring down the security gate over the storefront. Exiting through the store's back door, he set the alarm and climbed the stairs to his modest-one bedroom apartment. The thump of his cane marked each step.

Once inside the apartment, he set the dead bolt and made several phone calls, including one overseas. Then he pulled out his suitcase and began to pack.

Chapter 2

A bel paced the snug three-star hotel room, leaving a string of footprints in the plush beige carpet — to the bathroom, around two full-sized beds, back to the window — where he peeked out between the closed damask curtains to the alley below. His eyes followed the narrow stretch of asphalt to the avenue beyond, where he could see a few Parisians still strolling along the dim lane.

In the overseas phone call before his flight, he had been told where and what time to meet his contact. Though unsure what to expect, he vowed to follow the instructions. He owed that much to his family, especially after generations of holding onto the sketch in the hope the ring would surface.

Now it had.

He was a teenager when he first heard of the ring — a whispered conversation over a passed scrap of paper between his grandfather and father. They had shown him the sketch and asked him to memorize it. Then it was stored in the locked tin box in the safe. Even though his father had reminded him of it on his deathbed, it wasn't until he saw Julia's ring that the decades-old memory rocketed to the forefront of his mind.

Abel hiked the sleeve of his shirt to glance at his watch. Midnight. Time to go.

Thick, moist fog that engulfed the city shrouded Abel as he tugged at the collar of his brown leather jacket until it guarded his neck in defense. Fine droplets beaded on his glasses and clothes as the mist swirled around him. The rank odor of dust and smoke from fireplaces saturated the air. Through the heavy vapor illuminated only by streetlights, he could barely discern his surroundings. The late hour, the gloomy night, the monochrome setting, and the clandestine mission made him feel like a character in a film noir.

Rhythmic strides slapped at the damp sidewalk punctuated by the click of his cane. To ward off the night and anyone who might greet him with a friendly bonjour, he tucked his head into his jacket. After several blocks, he turned left at Voie Centrale and circled around to the back of a weathered stone building that engulfed his view, Eglise Catholique de Saint-Paul. A concrete sidewalk at the southern end of the property led him to a rusty wrought iron gate, which opened into the expansive yet cramped cemetery surrounding the church.

Abel stepped onto a stone walkway. The tap, tap, tap of his cane quickened as he passed a forest of marble headstones with carved crosses, bronze figures cast in elevated crypts, and elaborate family vaults as though his presence would disturb those lying there. Sure, he had visited the graves of his father, mother, and his beloved wife, Edna, in New York many times, but never in the dead of night, never in such gloom. Tonight's eerie setting made him feel as though things unseen were just around the next tombstone.

When he arrived at a weathered wooden door he paused, turned, and scanned the graveyard with great vigilance, at least what he could see of it through the stubborn fog. Yes, he was alone.

He rapped on the dark wood entry four times with his cane. Hesitation. Three more raps. The dull knocks punctured the silence of the night before being absorbed in the mist. From the other side of the door, he heard a man's muffled voice — English with a heavy French accent.

"There is no moon tonight."

"Obscured by the fog," Abel returned.

The door creaked open and a hint of incense wafted out. Just as Abel stepped across the threshold, a gust of humid wind whipped around him slamming the door shut and leaving him blinking in a dark alcove. A shiver shot through him.

"Come, let's talk by the fire," the voice said.

In silence, Abel felt a hand guide his arm through a doorway and down a corridor lit by a flickering glow. On his left, a door opened into a large room with a soaring ceiling where colorful frescos of cherry cheeked cherubs peered down at him. A wood fire crackled in a stone fireplace, shooting sparks into a wide chimney. Two facing brown leather wingback chairs with a small table in between sat on an oversized Persian rug in front of the fire.

The man gestured for Abel to take a seat. He felt the fire's heat on his face and was relieved to be out of the chilly, damp Paris night. He loosened the zipper on his jacket.

"Brandy?" the man asked.

"Yes," Abel answered, almost in a whisper. He watched the flames lick the air and cast eerie dancing shadows about the room. A floor lamp next to a roll top desk in one corner sent out a yellow glow illuminating floor-to-ceiling shelves with hundreds, maybe thousands, of books in what he assumed was the church library. Did each book hold a secret as significant as the one in his pocket?

The man handed Abel a crystal snifter containing reddish-gold liquor. The aroma of cherry bloomed in the transparent tumbler. The man took his seat. The fire's glow bounced off his sharp nose and chin, brown eyes, wrinkled face, and gray thinning hair. It was captured in his black cassock.

"I assume you have it with you?" The priest sipped his brandy.

"Yes." Abel patted the pocket of his jacket.

"May I see it?"

"Of course." Abel withdrew the white cardboard box and handed it to him.

The priest placed his snifter on the scalloped mahogany side table and lifted the lid. He removed the cotton batting and examined the ring with intensity.

"Is it the one?" Abel asked.

"It appears so, but you must read its history to understand its significance."

The priest placed the box on the side table and crossed to the bookshelves behind him. He positioned a rolling ladder and climbed to the seventh shelf, far above what a man could reach from the floor. The priest removed a cover of faux book spines made to look like books of differing heights and colors and reached into the space behind it. After withdrawing a large book, he replaced the cover and descended. He placed the book on the table between the chairs.

Abel had never seen such a book. It was the size of an old accounting ledger and bound in dark leather, much of it worn and cracked. The image of a falcon with outstretched wings was embossed on the front. He ran his calloused fingers over the rendering, feeling the peaks and

16

valleys of the impression as though he were a blind man reading brail.

"Why a falcon?" he asked.

"You'll understand what it denotes when you read the first chapter."

"It's all documented here?" Abel placed his palm on the worn book.

"It's taken me most of my life to put the pieces together. It's all there except what you've told me. I'll add that."

The book crackled as Abel opened it. His eyes grew wide as he took in the illumination on the first page, the Middle Ages craft of decorating manuscripts with intricate paintings. The main image was a vibrant, detailed picture of a diamond ring on a woman's hand. It was bordered by intricate gold scroll work and various colored flowers. The page was made of a translucent material, thin, and quite smooth, yet it appeared more durable than paper. Given the age of the image, could the medium be vellum, made from processed animal skin that preceded paper?

The woman's hand rested on a pillow of midnight blue velvet that accented her pale, dainty fingers. The exquisite ring and her rounded nails, filed short and buffed to a high shine, revealed a great deal about the woman — an aristocrat whose hands had never touched a dish pan or tended a garden. As Abel had seen a lot of hands in his days, he could predict with pronounced accuracy the age of his customers by the texture of their skin and whether they had knotted arthritic fingers, prominent veins, or brown age spots, despite cosmetic surgery performed on their faces or other parts of their bodies. To him, it was the hands that gave away a person's age. Abel concluded this hand belonged to a girl between fifteen and twenty.

While the depiction of the hand was lovely, it was the ring that absorbed Abel. A modest diamond encircled by six smaller ones perched atop a gold band that encircled the fourth finger of the woman's left hand. The coloration of the gems was painstakingly vivid with a masterful blending of a rainbow of colors, as though every facet of the diamonds' two-dimensional forms sparkled in a brilliant light. What artist had painted this exquisite image? The shading was as rich and meticulous as some contemporary digital images, but Abel knew it must have been painted centuries ago and taken weeks or even months to finish.

He turned the page.

The title of the book and the author's name were written in Old English in the center of the right page:

Women of the Ring
by
Father Albert Devereaux

Not a very imaginative title, but it described quite aptly what he was about to read.

"Is this where it all started?" Abel asked.

"Yes, and continued," Father Albert said. "But only you and I know how it will end. Take your time, read it all, but be warned: It could prove to be quite troubling. It may disturb you."

Abel acknowledged the warning with a slight nod. He took a swallow of brandy and felt the tepid alcohol trace a ribbon of heat down his throat, like one of the flames from the fire.

"I'll check back with you in a few hours." Father Albert picked up the ring box and crossed the room. At the threshold, he peered back at the jeweler. He bowed his head, made the sign of the cross, and quietly closed the door.

Chapter 3

The clatter of rattling metal rose into the Saturday morning air as Julia rapped on the security gate of Moody's Jewelry & Repair.

No response.

With cupped hands around her eyes, she peered through the grate to the store beyond. That's when she saw the scribbled note, Closed for Emergency, taped to the window. Inside, jewelry was displayed in the front window and cases as though business as usual, yet she could detect no lights or movement.

Abel's pointed questions about the ring still bothered her. Wasn't it sufficient that her grandmother had bequeathed it to her? Why was he so intent on its history? Maybe that type of history really was his hobby, but his line of questioning seemed a bit odd and gnawed at her.

"He didn't sound as though anything was wrong," Julia said to Winston, who stood next to her peering through the metal closure as well. "I just don't understand."

"Well, I don't know there's anything more you can do. He's not answering his cell phone, and you've left several messages at his store and home. Now we're here. I'm sure he'll be back well before the engagement party. We'll just have to wait." Winston, just taller than six feet with brown hair and equally brown eyes, squeezed Julia's hand.

"Well, I'd like to canvas the neighboring stores. Maybe they know something."

"I'll go with you."

The couple proceeded to speak with owners flanking Abel's store, plus several across the street — a bakery, shoe repair, market, and restaurant. No one was aware of his emergency. No one had seen or talked to him, though one proprietor thought he may have seen him getting into a taxi.

Julia's brow creased in worry. "It wouldn't be like him to disappear without telling someone. And the jewelry is still sitting in the window. He always stores it away in the safe before closing, so he wouldn't have left it there unless something urgent came up."

Winston sighed. "Let's give it a few more days. If you don't hear from him by then, we can call the police. Maybe they know something we don't."

"I'm sure you think this is just about making sure we have the ring for our engagement party, but it's not. Mr. Moody has been a very special person in my life. In fact, I wouldn't be who I am today if it weren't for him." Julia narrowed her eyes at Winston.

"This is the first time I've heard this. Mind telling me the story?"

"Let's get some coffee." Julia entwined her arm into Winston's and guided him down the sidewalk.

Named after Domino Chalky of Irish descent, Chalky's Pub beckoned at the corner of 86th Street and 20th Avenue. The white clapboard upper two stories housed Chalky's apartment while the first floor with black painted brick was the pub. In typical fashion, a long wooden bar dominated the dark interior with bistro tables and small cloth covered booths in a modern print snuggled against the outside wall. In one corner, a room with a dartboard and single pool table entertained some of the eclectic mix of patrons. Behind a back wall of glass, a brick patio sprinkled with white plastic tables offered alfresco seating when weather permitted. Today was not one of those days.

Julia and Winston grabbed a cozy booth away from the raucous crowd playing darts and pool. They ordered cappuccinos from the attentive server and unwrapped themselves, shedding coats, scarves, and gloves on the seat beside them.

"So what's the story?" Winston asked. "How did Mr. Moody help make you who you are?" He wrapped his hands around his coffee.

Julia picked up her cappuccino and blew across the top of the frothy white foam. Steam rose effortlessly into the air.

"It started when I stole a necklace."

Winston feigned a look of shock — eyes wide, mouth agape. "You? I'm engaged to a thief?"

Julia slapped his hand playfully.

"I was eight, and my father had just left us. Apparently, he wanted more excitement than my mother with three demanding children could give him. He constantly yelled that the house and we kids looked disheveled. I thought it was my fault because as the oldest I wasn't helping out enough. I felt ugly and became very angry. I acted out in school, was mean to the other kids.

"Mom coped the best she could, but Dad wasn't always on time with the child support. To earn extra money, she stayed late at the office and took a part-time job on Saturdays. Grandmother helped out by staying with us, but I missed my mother and father."

Winston squeezed Julia's hand across the table. "When I was growing up, Charlie, my best friend at school, was about your same age when his parents divorced. He had a rough time with it. His parents alternated custody on weekends, but he couldn't understand why they weren't a family anymore and wondered what he had done to cause his father to leave. It's hard for children to understand that separation and divorce are about their parents, not them."

"So true, especially in my case. One afternoon after school, I found myself in front of Mr. Moody's jewelry store. I'd been their dozens of times with my mother and grandmother for jewelry and watch repairs, but this time I was alone. I stood gawking at the sparkling necklaces in the window and wishing I was as beautiful. I felt certain that if I could wear one of the necklaces, I would become so beautiful that my father would come home and love me, my mother, and brothers. It was then that I decided to steal a necklace."

***

March 1994, Moody's Jewelry & Repair

"Why, Miss Julia, you're all by yourself. Where is your mother or grandmother?" Mr. Moody peered north and south down the street and across it but saw neither of her guardians.

"I don't need them. I'm big enough to go where I want." Julia scrunched her face and balled her fists on her hips.

"Well, so you are." Mr. Moody chuckled. "I see you're admiring the necklaces. Why not come in and see them up close?" He stepped aside and opened the door.

Julia bolted inside to the necklace case. She slapped her hands on the glass and pressed her nose against it, leaving oily imprints of all three.

"Look here, you can see them much better this way." Mr. Moody beckoned her behind the case equal to her

22

height. He unlocked the door in the back, slid it open, and pointed inside. "Which one do you want to see?"

Just then, the bell sounded at the front door, indicating a customer. Mr. Moody buzzed the lady through. "I'll be right back."

Julia didn't take her eyes off the glimmering necklaces as Mr Moody walked away. Which one would make her more beautiful? She fingered several but was drawn to a string of diamonds with a teardrop emerald pendant. She glanced over the counter on tiptoes to see that Mr. Moody was still talking to the lady then whisked the necklace from the case and into her skirt pocket.

Mr. Moody escorted the lady out and rounded the necklace case. "So, that's the one you picked? Why, that's a beautiful choice. Let's hook it around your neck and see how it looks."

Julia froze wide-eyed as Mr. Moody pulled the end of the diamond necklace dangling from her pocket. Without a word, he gently spun her around and clasped the band around her neck. He pushed a mirror on the countertop toward her and angled it so she could see herself.

Julia's fingers caressed the gleaming jewels as she stared at her reflection. The necklace made her look so . . . beautiful. Abel stepped back and crossed his arms. His eyes twinkled, and a smile lit up his face.

"The emerald matches your eyes. You look like a princess."

"Do you really think so?" Julia asked timidly.

"I sure do. One day, you'll own a necklace like this, but believe me, it won't be anywhere as beautiful as you. Here, let's take your photo."

Mr. Moody retrieved a camera from his back room and snapped a Polaroid. He handed the photo to Julia.

She bobbed her knees as she waited for it to develop, then stared at the image, captivated by what came to life in her hands.

"I have to close up shop now, Miss Julia, so we'll have to put the necklace away. But you can come back anytime and wear it." Mr. Moody unclasped the band from her neck and returned it to the case.

Julia left the store without a word, her eyes locked on the photo in a trance.

***

"Obviously, Mr. Moody knew I was stealing the necklace, but he never said a word." Julia sipped her cappuccino.

"So is that what you were referring to when you said he made you what you are today?" Winston asked.

"Partly. After that, I spent a lot of time in Mr. Moody's store, especially when I had a bad day at school or felt ugly. Mom knew where I was and was happy I had someone to look after me. He let me wear the necklace anytime I wanted, even with customers coming and going. He said I'd become a fixture in the store and that I was good for business because the customers loved seeing me model his jewelry. Being there made me feel better. What I didn't realize until years later is that I didn't feel better because I was wearing the necklace; it was because Mr. Moody took a genuine interest in me."

"Where's the necklace now?"

"Oh, Mr. Moody sold it several months later, but I still have the photo." Julia reached into her bag and withdrew the creased, faded image from her wallet. She handed it to Winston.

Julia stood like a statue in a dark-blue skirt and white blouse between the display cases. Her eyes were wide and her lips drawn into an unsure smile. The necklace, much too large for her, lay at an angle half-tucked under her shirt collar. Winston gazed from the photo of the girl to the woman beside him and back again.

"You haven't changed much." Winston laughed. "You still look like a princess. Only now, you sparkle just like the necklace." He kissed her softly on the cheek.

Julia returned the photo to her wallet. "I always keep the photo with me and pull it out whenever I have a bad day. It reminds me of that special afternoon, that things are never as bad as we think, and that God can turn every negative into a positive."

"How did you feel when Mr. Moody sold the necklace?"

Julia laughed. "Ah, that was the day I learned a most valuable lesson. But it's a story for another time. We need to get ready for the dinner tonight. We don't want to be late, right?"

CHAPTER 4

A bel pulled his chair closer to the fire and propped his feet on the hearth. Instead of being exhausted after the long trip and little sleep, he was wide awake aided by a surge of adrenaline in anticipation of what he was about to read.

With brandy in hand, he turned the page of the large book that covered his lap.

~~~

Mary of Burgundy

Mary slipped a long leather glove made of deerskin onto her right hand up to her elbow and opened the latch on the large wooden cage. Le Rapide, her two-year-old peregrine falcon peeked his head from the enclosure and hopped onto her gloved fist. With her left hand, Mary clipped one end of a thin leather strap to the bird's leg cuff and knotted the other end to a metal ring attached to the bottom of her glove. She withdrew a tiny leather hood from her waist pouch and slipped it over Le Rapide's head to cover his eyes. This would calm the bird until it was time for him to hunt.

"M'lady, are you ready? Shall I release the dogs?" The two white-and-brown Jack Russell terriers at Antoine's feet tugged at their leashes in eager anticipation.

"Not quite yet. I want to walk out farther."

The falcon, well over a foot in height, had round, alert, black eyes, matching yellow feet and beak, and a speckled underside with dark-gray flight feathers. Antoine had captured it as a yearling, and Mary had trained it under his tutelage. The undertaking had demanded at least fifteen hours of her time every week for several months, but Mary didn't mind. She had nurtured a special relationship with Le Rapide, and she loved taking him out of the mews and into the meadows to watch him soar. Eventually, she would release him back into the wild. Until then, the two would enjoy the excitement of the hunt together.

As the dry marsh crackled underfoot, Mary felt the tall yellow and brown grasses tug at her gray informal day dress and brunette braid that reached down her back past her waist. It was fall's dry season — the best time to find game birds grazing among the reeds. In the spring, the marsh brimmed with water, so hunting moved to higher fields.

Mary removed Le Rapide's hood and tether after some distance from the horses and wagon tied to a tree on a knoll at the field's edge. She circled her left hand, signaling to Antoine to release the dogs. Mary raised her glove, and Le Rapide pushed off her fist, flapped his broad wings, and took flight. She watched as he skimmed the ground before climbing higher and higher until he was just a dark speck against the afternoon's azure sky.

Several pheasants, flushed by the terriers, lit into the air. Mary watched as Le Rapide spotted their movement below with his keen vision and began to dive. He tucked his wings into his body and down, down he plunged, mimicking the speed of a projectile fired from a cannon. Just before intersecting with one of the pheasants, he spread his wings, extended his legs and grasped the fowl with his sharp talons in a forceful strike that killed the bird in mid-flight. Feathers flew from the game bird and floated in the air as pheasant and falcon spiraled to the ground.

Mary followed the tinkling of a bell attached to Le Rapide's leg and rushed toward the downed birds while Antoine recalled the dogs. When she arrived, the falcon's sharp, curved beak was yanking feathers from the pheasant. Mary withdrew a scrap of fresh duck meat from a second waist pouch and tucked it into her gloved hand. She extended it toward the raptor, and Le Rapide hopped onto her glove to tear at it.

Just steps behind Mary, Antoine stuffed the expired pheasant into a large basket he had slung over his shoulder. "M'lady, how many more would you like to get?"

"At least two." She tethered the falcon back onto her glove and slipped the hood over his eyes to ready him for his second flight.

Mary sent her afternoon kill to the galley for preparation for the night's dinner. Her home, the ducal Castle of Coudenberg, was perched on a hill overlooking Brussels. Built in 1100 by the counts of Leuven and Brussels, it initially was constructed as part residence, part primary defense and was later included in the first great wall built around Brussels in 1152. The castle was converted to a palatial residence when the second wall was built following the occupation by Louis II of Flanders in 1346. Charles the

Bold, Mary's father, took up residence in the castle in 1467 when he was named Duke of Burgundy.

As Mary entered the castle foyer, her father rushed to her side.

"Where have you been? You've been keeping Ferdinand of Aragon waiting." His face flushed and his eyes stern, Charles shadowed his daughter through the spacious entry toward the stone staircase.

"He's early, Father, just like he was the first time. Besides, I find him ill-mannered and crude. Send him away." Mary flicked her hand in dismissal as she climbed the stairs to her room. Her father continued to trail her as portraits of ancestors dressed in royal regalia and encased in ornate gilded frames peered down at them with faces that appeared chiseled from rough wood. Though their mouths were closed, their eyes spoke of disapproval at Mary's rude treatment of the potential suitor.

"My daughter, I know you're not fond of those who have called on you thus far, but you can't wait forever to make a decision. The duchy's very future depends upon the political bond forged by your marriage. You must make your selection."

Mary took a deep breath as she turned to her father on the landing. She cupped his face in her hands and kissed his cheek tenderly.

"Dear father, I am surely aware of my duties as your daughter to the legacy of the duchy, the land you so fiercely fight to protect, but am I not entitled to a little happiness along the way? Pray father, would you have me marry without a hint of affection for the man that would share my bed and begat your grandchildren, heirs to the duchy?" Her sixteen-year-old hazel eyes searched her father's for understanding as she pleaded her case.

Mary knew that her future rested in her father's hands and that her marriage would be used to protect the duchy, family fortune, and further her father's political ambitions. After all, these types of marriages had been arranged for centuries, just as her parent's marriage. She also understood that her father's reign and that of her grandfather had been retained through fierce battles with neighboring monarchs. As well, she was abundantly aware of the wives' roles in running the duchies and raising money to fortify the territories against their enemies when their husbands were engaged in long battles. True, the wives fulfilled significant, noble roles, but Mary wanted something more from her marriage than mere duty.

Her schooling had been the best available. Mary's mother, Isabella, daughter of the Duke of Bourbon, a neighboring duchy, ensured she began her education in the arts early. At age eight, Mary had become an accomplished pianist, artist, and chess player just before her mother's death from tuberculosis. So doted on was she by her parents and subsequently her stepmother that she had been afforded every amenity of the age. Her grandmother, Isabel of Portugal, had indulged her affinity for animals by gifting her at age ten with a menagerie of monkeys and parrots to complement her collection of dogs and a giraffe. It was in outdoor activities, however, where Mary truly came alive.

One of her favorite pastimes was skating on the frozen ponds around the castle, and she excelled in hunting, riding, and falconry. With her attributes augmented by the wealth of the duchy, Mary had become the most eligible heiress in Europe, thereby attracting myriad suitors.

"Very well," Charles said, yielding to his daughter's wishes regarding the suitor. "But the archduke arrives in three days." His rigid stare imparted a silent demand for

Mary's certain presence at this visit, a directive she dare not dismiss.

Jeanne de Clito, formally called Lady Hallewijn, hiked up her skirt and ran up a gauntlet of stairs to Mary's room. Gasping for breath, she selected a carved wooden fan from Mary's dresser and waved it frantically at her face.

"He's here," she finally uttered upon catching her breath. A cousin of Mary's, Jeanne had been her constant companion since Mary was a small child.

Mary stood in front of a full-length mirror taking in her reflection. Her petite frame, just taller than five feet, entertained an oval face accented by a small nose. Brunette hair and her most outstanding feature of hazel eyes stood out against her porcelain skin. Her braided hair, piled high on her head, was receiving the final touch of a jeweled comb by her lady-in-waiting.

"Well, now that you're finished your spying, Lady Hallewijn, do tell me what is this one like?" Despite the courtly regimen with a string of eligible suitors, this would be her first time meeting the archduke, even though her father had begun preliminary marriage negotiations with his family when she was a mere child.

"Overall, quite attractive. He's tall and blond. A little thin, perhaps, but his muscles appear taught. His nose is a bit hooked, but his eyes are a soft brown, kind, and quite alert."

Mary adjusted her olive-green embroidered dress. It would be modest, yet elegant for Maximilian, Archduke of Austria from the House of Habsburg, one of the most influential royal houses of Europe and through which the Holy Roman Empire was continuously occupied. Should she and Maximilian marry, it would be a coup for both families. Maximilian's father, Frederick III, had been concerned about Burgundy's tendencies to expand its territory on the western border of his empire, and he and her father had been at odds for decades. Mary's union to Maximilian would forestall any further political or military conflict between the rulers.

"Tell me about his countenance. I'm much more interested in that," Mary said.

Jeanne cleared her throat and spoke in a soft, unflinching voice. "He exudes confidence, and his lips are well-spoken. His voice is strong, and his laugh rings true. But it's his smile, Mary. It's one that could melt the cruelest heart."

Mary grinned. "Well, that's a good start. We'll see about the rest."

Mary was surprised to find Maximilian well-educated and charming, despite being two years her junior. He spoke seven languages, and the two discovered they shared a love of hunting and falconry.

After several days together, Mary felt sure she and Maximilian would wed, but knew marriage treaties took several years with much posturing and negotiating between the families. Dowries, land, and ruling legacies needed to be considered. And, of course, the Catholic Church, which was intimately involved in all royal marriages, had to give its blessing.

Mary and Maximilian met several times during the next four years while their fathers worked out the details of the marriage proposal. As reinforcement, Mary arranged to send Maximilian a ring, which with his acceptance would become her engagement ring. She and her father called upon a merchant from India to find the perfect stone for the band and chose an uncut diamond. They selected Louis Van Berquem, a Flemish goldsmith and jeweler in Paris, to cut and mount the gem. He had invented a technique of cutting and faceting that guaranteed it would "release the reflective properties of the natural diamond crystal." Mary was greatly impressed with the result — a gold band with an exquisite center diamond surrounded by six smaller ones.

Before Mary, now twenty, could send the ring to Maximilian, she received word that her father had met his untimely death in the Battle of Nancy against the Swiss Confederacy and Rene II, Duke of Lorraine. She was heartbroken, but more than that, she knew her father's death would deal a serious blow to the duchy of Burgundy. Now, more than ever, it was imperative for her to finalize her marriage treaty to Maximilian to retain lands and protect the people.

With haste, she sent a letter to the archduke along with the diamond ring as her pledge. In April, emissaries arrived back at the Coudenberg castle with Maximilian's reply. Mary held her breath as she opened the letter.

"What does it say?" Jeanne asked, resting her chin on Mary's shoulder and peering at the archduke's response.

Mary sighed in relief. "He's accepted my proposal and has returned the ring." She slipped it onto the fourth finger of her left hand.

Two days later, Mary married Maximilian by proxy because he was still in Austria. Four months later when he arrived at the castle on August 18, they were formally married in a small ceremony the same day.

Mary loved the diamond ring and wore it every day. It symbolized a union that was not only profitable for the duchy but for her as well, as she and Maximilian grew to deeply love each other, even sharing a bedroom, something that at the time was quite foreign for married couples.

The two taught each other languages; Mary taught Maximilian French while he taught her German. They spent their days governing and hunting and their nights cuddled in bed reading romances. They eventually had three children: Philip the Handsome in 1478, Margaret in 1480, and Franz in 1481.

Mary was thrilled to have a new son in the castle, but Franz didn't take to feeding like her other children and struggled to gain weight.

"He's so frail, Jeanne, not at all robust like the others, and he never cries. Now he won't take my breast even though I know he's hungry. Something's wrong."

Mary rocked Franz back and forth in her arms and spoke softly to the boy. All the while, his eyes remained closed and his body listless.

"Shall I call for the doctor?" Jeanne looked from the child to Mary whose face was covered in worry.

"Please, though I'm afraid the child may not last until he arrives."

Jeanne rushed out the door and returned several minutes later. Mary looked up as she entered the room. Tears streamed down her cheeks as she cradled her lifeless son.

"Oh, Mary!" Jeanne said. She burst into tears and covered her face with her hands.

In the days that followed, Mary hardly got out of bed or ate. While she attended her son's funeral, it sapped every ounce of her strength. To add to her woes, Maximilian was called away to fight King Louis XI in defense of the duchy. Whatever energy Mary could muster was devoted to prayer and rearing the children, but her depression became more pronounced.

Eventually, peace prevailed in the surrounding countryside, and Mary received word of Maximilian's return in the spring of 1482. For days, she paced in front of the window watching for him. When she finally saw him approach, she dashed from the castle and flung herself into his arms. It was more energy than she had conjured in three months.

"My love, I'm so glad you're home." Mary planted kisses on her husband's face.

Maximilian held her tightly and returned the affection. "I can't tell you how much I've missed you and the children." After a prolonged hug, he wrapped his arm around her waist and guided her into the castle.

The two spent the next day in seclusion. Then it was back to duchy business as usual for Maximilian, but not for Mary. While she was delighted to have her husband home, still she languished. Several days later, she was sitting in the drawing room when Antoine asked to see her.

"Please, m'lady, in celebration of the archduke's return, allow me to arrange a hunt. I'm sure it will raise your spirits."

Mary declined at first but then relented. "Perhaps you're right, Antoine. Please ready our horses and the falcons."

"Very well, m'lady. It will be good to see you two together again on the marshes." Antoine smiled, bowed and made his way to the stable to prepare for the hunt.

Mary changed into her hunting clothes, and she and Maximilian met Antoine in front of the castle. Antoine helped her sit aside her horse with both legs to her left, allowing the folds of her skirt to cover her legs in modesty. Despite the crude sidesaddle, which was not designed for comfort or stability, Mary learned to gallop without falling by clinging tightly and shifting her weight.

The ride to the fields took the couple through the forest along an elevated path wide enough for two horse-drawn carts traveling side-by-side. Antoine drove behind the couple in the wagon, which accommodated the terriers and the crates of falcons. Periodically, the sun peeked between the billowing clouds, yet the March spring air remained quite cool, and a brisk breeze swayed the trees that had yet to leaf. Phacelia covered the forest floor in a blanket of white, and an earthy scent permeated the air as the rich moist earth gave way to new spring grasses and vegetation.

Mary lifted her face to the sun and smiled as she rode beside Maximilian. Breathing in the clean, crisp air, and being among the sun-dappled aspens she so loved gave her a feeling as warm as the sun on her face.

"Antoine was right, I do feel better," she said.

"I'm so glad," Maximilian said. "The castle was probably a gloomy place this winter after Franz's death and my being gone so long. I'm sure Philip and Margaret were a comfort, but it takes fresh air in your lungs to truly make you feel alive."

"So true, my love. Race you to the marsh?"

After the hunt, Antoine led the way in the cart with the dogs, the birds, and the downed game. Mary and Maximilian followed on their horses twenty yards back. Without warning, a rogue gust of wind howled through the forest sending trees twisting over the pathway. Seconds later, the couple heard a loud crack. A large dead tree thudded to the ground in front of them and blocked their path.

The horses neighed, reared, and became frantic as they sought escape from the monstrous wooden carcass. Maximilian reined in his horse, but Mary was unable to control hers. With eyes flashing, it circled wildly and reared a second time. Clouds and trees swirled above Mary in a dizzying blur as she plummeted to the ground. Stunned by the fall and with her breath knocked from her, she watched helplessly as her frenzied thousand-pound equine lost its footing on the muddy soil and fell backward. Her shriek echoed throughout the woodland as the horse landed on her.

Through excruciating pain and blurred vision, Mary watched the horse quickly right itself and dart down the path away from the fallen tree trunk. Then she passed out. She regained consciousness just before the doctor arrived at the castle but refused to be examined because of modesty. For days, she lay in unbearable pain, unable to move her legs. With the outward diagnosis a broken back accompanied by multiple internal injuries, at age twenty-five, Mary knew her death was imminent.

"My love, please bring me the children. I want to say goodbye." Mary's pale form blended into the white bed sheets, contrasted only by her brunette hair that cascaded around her like water.

Maximilian, who had remained at her bedside day and night, had Philip and Margaret brought into the room. Mary bade the children goodbye, kissing each tenderly and transferring her tears to their soft cheeks. Maximilian knelt at Mary's bedside when the children and staff left the room.

"I cannot bear to live without you," he said. Tears flowed from his eyes as he caressed his cherished wife's hand and stroked her colorless cheeks. "You are my beloved, and there will never be anyone else." He planted a soft kiss on her pale lips.

Mary swept back a lock of blond hair from his forehead. "My husband, I have loved you with unfailing affection, and you have given me immense joy. While I can no longer be with you, please keep this as a reminder of our love." Mary removed the precious diamond ring from her trembling hand and pressed it into Maximilian's. "Take care, my love, until I see you again in God's glorious kingdom of heaven."

~~~

Abel rested his head against the wingback and drained his snifter as the grandfather clock in the corner chimed 4:00 a.m. He hadn't even heard the previous chimes. Just then, Father Albert entered the room.

"Tired yet?" he asked.

Abel looked up from the book. "Actually, that first chapter kept me quite awake."

"As will the others. Here, I brought you a snack." Father Albert placed a small tray on the side table laden with glass of red wine, a bottle of water and a variety of French wheat crackers and cheeses — Roquefort, Camembert, and Brie. "I'll be back in the morning, and we'll have a full breakfast."

"Before you leave, Father, can you tell me what happened to Maximillian and the ring? I'm sure he was heartbroken over his wife's death."

Father Albert sat down with a sigh.

"He was. Mary was buried in the cemetery outside the Church of Our Lady in Bruges, Flanders, but later Maximillian had her reinterred in a gilded bronze effigy and laid to rest next to her father inside the same church. In devotion to her, he kept her ring in an opened cherry wood box on his dresser. Seeing it every day, however, brought him immense heartache. Two years after her death, he sent the ring back to Louis, the jeweler in Paris, accompanied by a note: 'Please sell the ring when you can and return the proceeds.'

"Once the aristocracy received word that Mary's ring was in Louis's shop, they flocked to see it, having heard of its uniqueness and unparalleled beauty. Yet the viewings failed to return one sale, let alone sincere interest, despite the exquisite craftsmanship and sparkle of the diamonds. Maximilian was told that women felt the ring was cursed because Mary had died so tragically while wearing it."

"So no one bought the ring?"

Father Albert shook his head. "Rumor of the curse was too widespread."

"So, what happened to it?" Abel leaned in.

"Maximilian ascended to Holy Roman emperor at age twenty-seven in 1519. Louis, however, still had an obligation to find a solution for the ring. His apprentice from Tanzania, a man named Masego, had shown exceptional skill in jewelry design and craftsmanship. One day, he approached Louis and suggested just the resolution he was looking for. He showed Louis a sketch of the ring he had redesigned with a ten carat blue African sapphire in the central position.

"Around the sapphire would be the smaller diamonds from Mary's ring and darker blue sapphires. Each triangular gap between these would be filled with gold overlaid with dark-blue enamel. To honor the duchess's memory, he would paint a small symbol in gold on each enamel triangle depicting a falcon in flight. No one except Louis and Masego would know that the diamonds were from Mary of Burgundy's original ring."

"And now we know," Abel said. "Did Louis ever sell the ring?"

"Ah, you'll have to read the next chapter to find that out." Father Albert rose and crossed the room. As before, he gave the sign of the cross before leaving.

Abel was about to turn to the next chapter when he noticed a sticky note at the bottom of the page in Father Albert's handwriting:

Mary's original ring was the first diamond engagement ring in history and began centuries of tradition.

Chapter 5

"How'd you like the dinner tonight?" Julia asked from the passenger's seat of Winston's gold BMW X2 parked at the curb in front of her apartment.

"Your mom outdid herself," Winston said. "The get-together couldn't have gone more smoothly."

Julia's mother had invited Winston's parents over for a pre-engagement dinner and to finalize plans for the party. It would be a grand affair on the terrace of the William Vale hotel overlooking the Hudson River. Employees at Winston's app company, talented musicians in their own right, had offered to provide the music as an engagement gift.

"I agree, it certainly was one of her best dinners. And the company wasn't bad either." Julia winked at Winston. "I so wish Grandmother could have been there. She would have loved putting in her two cents' worth."

"Don't know what your grandmother would have said, but here's my two cents. How about the rest of your story? You know, when Mr. Moody sold the necklace?"

"Come on up for coffee, and I'll tell you all about it."

After making the coffee, Julia brought in a cup for Winston who sat on her Lovesac sectional. She settled next to him.

"I remember it as though it was yesterday," she said in a solemn tone. "It was a Saturday morning. I was turning nine the next week and was hoping Mr. Moody would give me the necklace for my birthday."

***

May 1994, Moody's Jewelry & Repair

"Where is it? Where is it? Where's my necklace?"

Julia ran from case to case in a frantic search for the diamond-and-emerald necklace to which she had grown attached. She opened the doors of each case, peered inside, and ran her hand across the velvet necklace busts knocking them out of the way in her wild hunt. Mr. Moody watched the commotion from the threshold of his workroom. When she finally stopped, all out of breath, he spoke in a calm tone.

"I sold it."

From the middle of the room, Julia drew herself up to her full height, puckered her brow, and balled her fists at her side. With a flushed face, she shot Mr. Moody a fiery stare.

"You sold it? You sold it? How could you do that? It was *mine!*" Julia shouted.

"Was it?" Mr. Moody said softly. "Was the necklace really yours?"

Julia opened her mouth, but no words flew out as the truth washed over her like a tsunami. Melting into a puddle, she blinked twice and burst into tears.

"But I won't be beautiful anymore without the necklace." Her sobs saturated every corner of the store.

Mr. Moody squatted to the floor and rocked Julia against him in his arms.

"Thing is, Miss Julia, you didn't need the necklace to be beautiful. You're already beautiful. You just needed the necklace to show you what was already inside." He pointed at her heart.

"I don't understand." Julia rubbed her eyes and smeared tears down her cheeks. Mr. Moody withdrew a handkerchief from his pants pocket and handed it to her.

"See, it isn't what's on the outside that makes you beautiful. No siree. It's what's on the inside. Do you remember when you came to my shop so many months ago? You were angry and . . . well . . . not so beautiful. But when you put on the necklace, you believed you were beautiful, so you acted beautiful. It wasn't really the necklace that made you beautiful; you became beautiful by thinking differently. When you did that, other things changed too. Why, look at how you've raised your grades and how much happier you are. Look at how many customers have left this store with joy in their hearts because they met you."

Julia froze, contemplating Mr. Moody's words. "You mean if I want things to be different, all I have to do is change how I think about them?" Julia wiped her eyes and nose with the handkerchief.

"That's only the first step, but it's a good start."

"What's the second one?"

"You have to put those thoughts changes into practice, just like you did. Once you thought the necklace made you beautiful, you wanted to show others your beauty, so you smiled, treated them kindly, and worked harder in school. You changed on the outside, but it started with changing your way of thinking."

"But I tore up your store looking for the necklace. I thought it was the necklace that made me beautiful."

"Yes, and that happens sometimes. You see, things don't really belong to people; people belong to things."

Julia cocked her head to one side and looked up at Mr. Moody. "That doesn't make any sense. Isn't this your store? Doesn't it belong to you?"

"Yes, that's true in a legal sense, but what I mean is that I try not to make it number one in my life. After all, I can't take it with me at the end of my life. Can't take my workbench. Can't take my cash register. Can't take the cases full of jewelry. We need to view ourselves more as keepers of the things we possess. Otherwise, those things wind up possessing us."

"Like the necklace and me? Like me believing I could only be beautiful because of the necklace?"

"That's right, Miss Julia. For most of us, it isn't a necklace. It might be a house, our job, car, even our children. We define who we are by our possessions, what we look like, what our job is, or who we're married to. But the good book says, 'A man becomes a slave to that which masters him.' Do you understand?"

"Uh, sort of."

"Well, the important thing is that you try to not let things master your life. Now, I want to show you something." Mr. Moody lifted Julia from his lap and rose from the floor using his cane for support. He retrieved a piece of paper from his workroom and handed it to Julia.

"What's this?" she asked.

"It's a check." Mr. Moody pointed at the "Pay to the Order of" line at the top. "See, that's your name, Julia Townsend. The check is made out to you."

"Me, why?"

"It's your commission on the sale of the necklace. The man who bought it told me it was because of you that he selected it for his wife. It's only fair that you reap some of the proceeds."

"Was it Mr. Evertson, the one whose daughter died?"

"Yes."

"I thought so. He was nice but seemed so sad."

"He said you reminded him of his daughter and that you touched him with your smile and friendliness. He said that while he thinks of his daughter every day, he will think of you too whenever his wife wears the necklace. So, you see, even though you'll miss the necklace, you're playing a huge part in making someone else very happy. You should be proud, Miss Julia."

Her eyes grew wide at the check. "I don't even have a bank account."

"Well, perhaps you should open one."

***

Winston took the coffee cups to the kitchen, where he washed them and angled them in the drainer.

"It must have been a big check," he said.

"Eight thousand dollars. That check and the money it earned over fifteen years in the stock market paid for my college education. I didn't even have to take out a student loan."

"Wow, that was incredibly nice."

"Yes, it was, but I left Mr. Moody's that day with something much more valuable than the check."

Chapter 6

Abel cut a small slice of Brie and spread it on a wheat cracker, grateful for the snack. He always enjoyed good cheeses and nothing was better than this – fresh, local cheese. He had learned to appreciate cheese through his father, who savored a plate of cheese and crackers and a glass of beer every night after work.

After a couple more bites and several sips of wine, Abel was ready to settle back in. He turned the page.

~~~

Catherine de' Medici

Catherine de' Medici, queen of France, looked out onto the courtyard from the upstairs window. Her pale skin, deep-set brown eyes, and brown hair, which was woven into a braid atop her head, contrasted nicely with her bronze-and-red embroidered dress.

Its neckline of layered white lace ruffles was accented with puffed sleeves flowing to her wrists and ending in ruffles. The ruffles, an element the queen designed to hide her double chin, was soon embraced as fashionable. The bodice of her dress, embellished with pearls, rubies, and other precious gems, hugged in her ample waistline. A teardrop crystal pendant dangled at the bust line. Perhaps it was an omen.

Liliana, the queen's lady-in-waiting, stood by her side at the window. "My Queen, aren't you going to the lists to watch King Henry joust with the Count of Montgomery?"

"Yes, of course. We will leave shortly. In the meantime, please have Hugo come up."

"Very well, Madame." Liliana gave her queen a slight bow of the head.

Catherine wore a ruby ring on her left hand and a sapphire ring on her right pinky. She had purchased the ring from Louis, a Paris jeweler, while searching for a broach for her daughter, Marguerite. The light blue sapphire, encircled by diamonds and darker-blue sapphires, had caught her fancy. Now with nervous precision, she twisted the ring around her plump little finger as though it would ease her angst.

"My Queen, how may I serve you?" Hugo said. He had been Catherine's most trusted advisor for over twenty years; ever since she married Henry at age fourteen in 1533. Back then, Henry was monarch of the House of Valois and second in line for the French throne after his older brother, Francis III, Duke of Brittany. However, Henry became heir apparent when Francis died at age eighteen from a suspected poisoning.

"Tell me, what's the latest regarding the Huguenots?" Catherine asked.

"Their numbers are growing every day, and their influence is spreading throughout Europe. It won't be long before they become a grave threat," Hugo said, not wanting to alarm the queen, yet give her an honest assessment.

In earlier conversations with Hugo, she had been told that the Huguenots had become a movement in 1521, just two years after her birth. Initiated by John Calvin, a Frenchman, and Martin Luther, a German and former monk, the movement began as a protest against the Catholic-dominated Europe and was designed to offer an alternative to the Roman Catholic Church. Separately, Calvin and Luther had encouraged Catholics to break ties with the Church and adopt new methods of Christian worship focusing on the central importance of Biblical texts and a personal relationship with God. People saw new hope in having direct access to God through Jesus, instead of saints or the church as the sole intercessors. Those involved in the movement became a widespread group of European citizens who banded together in faith. They were called Protestants.

"We must watch them closely," Catherine said. "Why, do you know I heard that Luther had the audacity to nail a copy of his 'Disputation on the Power and Efficacy of Indulgences' to the door of the All Saints' Church in Wittenberg? He's insisting that since forgiveness is God's alone to grant, buying indulgences cannot absolve one from consequences of sin or grant salvation. This philosophy alone would weaken the coffers of some churches that rely heavily on this income.

"As well, the movement has attracted the middle class and skilled artisans from all of Europe who believe the Catholic Church is a corrupt machine that wields too much power. This kind of thinking has put them at direct odds with the papacy and their movement now threatens the stability of Europe. More hostilities already have broken out, and tension looms over the region like a dark billowing cloud. Mark my words, Hugo, any day now the storm will let loose its fury."

Hugo shook his head. "It is inevitable. Anything else, Madame?"

"Yes, please have the carriage brought around, as I wish to go see my husband compete in the tournament."

"Very well, Your Majesty." Hugo gave his queen a bow before departing to fulfill her directive.

When Catherine arrived at the arena for the games, she smiled and waved to the glittering array of lords and ladies decked out in their finest regalia. They had come to watch the men compete in a variety of physical competitions. Catherine's smile quickly faded once settled into the king's box, though. In the next box over sat her nemesis, Diane de Poitiers, her husband's courtesan and chief mistress.

Catherine knew of Diane. It was common knowledge — even accepted — that royal, noble, and wealthy men dallied with one or numerous paramours. These men housed and clothed their lovers, lavished them with expensive jewelry, escorted them to royal events, and even valued their opinions on occasion. These women weren't commoners. They were well educated, sophisticated, charming women who typically worked their way up into the nobility of the ruling class, exchanging their companionship and sexual favors for the better attributes of life. These courtesans considered their profession a career, moving from one man to the next.

Yet, despite Catherine's loathing for her husband's mistress, she knew she could cope. She had endured far more difficult situations. Born the daughter of an Italian prince of the Medici family, a ruthless political dynasty, she never knew her mother. She had died of puerperal fever, a uterine infection, just days after giving birth to Catherine. A week later, Catherine's twenty-seven-year-old father died of consumption and left her an orphan.

She spent her youth in the care of her father's relatives, who included Popes Leo X and Clement VII, her uncles. She remembered it as a stormy time dominated by the Italian Wars, a struggle for power and territory among the various Italian families, including her own. In 1527, a German army under the authority of the Holy Roman Emperor Charles V sacked Rome. During this eclipse of Medici power, citizens of Florence took her hostage. She was only eight. It was traumatic even though she wasn't harmed. Eventually, Uncle Clement directed mercenaries to rescue her from a nunnery. Once safe, he set about finding her a suitable husband.

At age fourteen, suitors lined up for Catherine's hand, but Francis I of France won out when he proposed his second son, Henry, Duke de Orleans. She married Henry on October 28, 1533, in an elaborate ceremony conducted by the pope. At midnight, Catherine and Henry left the wedding ball to consummate their marriage.

It was during their first year of marriage that Henry took Diane, twenty years his senior, as his mistress. She became the most influential person in his life, a position he flaunted before the entire French court. The fact that Catherine was unable to bear children the first decade of their marriage made matters worse and diminished her popularity in the court. To counter her barrenness, she turned to astrologers and became a patroness of the seer Nostradamus. Remarkably, she birthed her first child, Francis II, in 1544. Nine others followed. This, she believed, was due to her indulgence in astronomy, astrology, and necromancy, the practice of communicating with the dead, especially to predict the future.

Though Catherine sat far too near her rival at the games, she nevertheless enjoyed the competition and thought it a fine spectacle of horsemanship, physical prowess, and gamesmanship. King Henry, forty, proved quite fit, though the Count of Montgomery of the king's Scots Guard, a highly trained company of men who served as the king's bodyguards, almost unseated him during their joust.

After the games, Catherine went to meet Henry in the tent where the athletes prepared. When she got there, she expected him to be ready to attend the post games celebration. Instead, he was still dressed in his jousting armor and about to head back onto the field. Although she could tell the king was physically spent, he refused to leave the games without solidifying his proficiency with the lance one more time with a final challenge to the count.

"Please, Henry, this isn't necessary," Catherine pleaded. "You won the joust, and the games are almost over. You have nothing more to prove. Even the count respectively declines your invitation. Besides, you're exhausted."

"Nonsense, I'm fine! I must maintain my dignity." He tucked his mental helmet under his arm and strode off in his plated armor and mail gloves.

Catherine squeezed back tears of frustration as he dismissed her advice and passed by his dressing table where he picked up a ribbon with Diane's colors. He would tie it around his lance, a gesture that showed for whom he rode and dedicated the joust. Catherine felt deeply wounded but forced herself to hold her head high on the return to her seat.

The horses snorted and pranced, nervous in their rider's two-colored banners of an alternating diamond motif that covered their entire bodies — blue and white for the king, green and yellow for the count. King Henry waited on his stallion at one end of the lists with his lance and shield, while Count Montgomery, equally equipped, sat on his stallion at the opposite end.

The trumpeters sounded the call and the official referee dropped the handkerchief to signal the start. The horses galloped toward each other as their horsemen lowered blunt-tipped lances until they pointed at their opponent.

Catherine sighed in relief when the wooden lances glanced off each shield in the first pass. However, in the second pass, Montgomery's lance shattered against Henry's helmet and lodged a long splinter in the king's left eye. Every spectator jumped up in a unified gasp as Henry grabbed his bloody helmet and swooned. There was a collective moan as he fell from his horse and landed on his back.

Catherine rushed onto the field, almost tripping as her long dress caught the grass. She reached Henry just as half a dozen men placed him on a stretcher and carried him to the first-aid tent for a preliminary assessment. Catherine realized he needed a surgeon and had him transferred to his apartment in the Chateau de la Tournelle, where the royal surgeon, Ambroise Paré, conducted a more thorough examination. Tearful and anxious, she stood by the king's side as the surgeon delivered the news — the splinter had pierced the king's brain, and other splinters had punctured his head and throat. While he had removed these, unfortunately, he could not halt the profuse internal bleeding.

Upon hearing Henry had only hours to live, Count Montgomery begged to address the king. Catherine was incensed at the tasteless appeal from the man she held responsible for her husband's sure death. Still lucid but fading, the king granted the audience.

Catherine gritted her teeth at the threshold of the room and watched Count Montgomery kneel at the king's bedside. Henry's skin manifested a sickly ashen color, and the aura of imminent death permeated the room like a dense fog.

"My king, take my hand and even my head for such an egregious offense," the count said, his head lowered. "Just say the word, sir."

Henry opened his good eye and tilted his face to the count. "Sir, I won't hear of this," he said in barely a whisper. "The fault is not yours. You carried yourself bravely and well. You are forgiven."

But Catherine did not forgive the Count. Through tears and bloodshot eyes, she threw darts of enmity at his back as he exited the room. She then took up vigil by her husband's bed, allowing no one to enter, especially Diane. Later that night, the royal priest administered last rites.

Catherine remained by Henry's bedside, staring at him. His placid face swept her back to their first year of marriage, when, in their youth, they explored each other with tenderness and wanting. He was gentle then, considerate. She smiled at the sweet memory. But his gasp soon jerked her back to reality.

It was his last.

She kissed his lips lovingly and wept.

The next day, Catherine sat on the throne in her receiving room and twisted the blue sapphire ring on her pinky. "Bring me Diane," she commanded.

"Yes, Madame," Hugo said.

Guards flanked Diane as she entered the room. Her head was down and her hands entwined in front of her. She stopped before the royal throne. What was once a visage of blithe haughtiness had been reduced to a whimper as she trembled before the queen. Catherine looked upon the sorrowful creature below her with a mixture of piety and pity.

"You have caused me unbearable grief during my marriage, and now the duty of the king's office falls squarely onto me until my son is crowned his successor. Therefore, by the power vested in me, you are banned from this court for life. You will return all jewels that Henry gave you, and you shall live out your remaining days in exile. Take her away!"

Catherine commanded Diane's exit with the wave of her royal hand. She smirked as the guards led her away.

Francis II, Catherine's oldest son, was crowned king at age fifteen. Her joy at his ascent was short lived, though, when less than a year later he died from a brain abscess caused by an ear infection. Charles IX, Catherine's second son, followed as king at age ten in 1560. Catherine became regent because of his young age. By proxy, she presided over the council, initiated and controlled state business, directed domestic and foreign policy, and made appointments to offices. In essence, she ruled France in his name until he was old enough to reign at thirteen and a half. Yet, she remained a controlling influence throughout his sovereignty, often conducting business in his name.

Catherine peered out the drawing room window of the Tuileries Palace to the Seine, where boats navigated the river. The ring went round and round on her little finger.

"Hugo, I hear of more unrest with the Huguenots, more altercations between the Protestants and Catholics."

"Yes, Madame. The number of causalities increases every day."

"We must try to keep peace. We must try to understand what these people want. Please arrange for me to meet with the Huguenot leaders. Perhaps we can find some common ground."

"It won't be easy to keep the pope and the people happy while trying to placate the Protestants. It appears you will be walking a narrow ledge and will be devoured no matter which way you fall."

"Indeed, it is a precarious line that I walk, but I have no choice. The country's future depends upon how much freedom France can give these rebellious Huguenots and still keep them under control."

"I've heard that Count Montgomery has left the church, that he's joined the movement and is now a Protestant."

"Yes, I've heard that too. His time will come." Catherine licked her lips as though she could taste the retribution already.

In 1562, civil war broke out in France, initiated by religious differences. In hopeful reconciliation and to appease both Catholics and Protestants after years of unrest, in 1572, Catherine arranged for her nineteen-year-old daughter, Marguerite, to marry a Protestant — Henry, King of Navaree. The wedding, to be held in Paris, was the byproduct of a matrimonial treaty negotiated by the papacy.

"Is everything in place?" Catherine asked.

"All arrangements have been made," Hugo said.

"Very well then. It should be a stirring event." A sardonic smile etched its way across Catherine's lips.

Hugo returned the grin. "No doubt, my queen."

Catherine saw to it that the marriage was an extravagant affair. They orchestrated celebrations throughout Paris days before and after the ceremony, which were attended by French royalty. Admiral Gaspard II de Coligny, the Huguenots leader, and other nobility in the growing Protestant movement also attended the festivities.

Four days after the wedding, Admiral Coligny was wounded in an assassination attempt while he was still in Paris. Huguenot leaders, livid at this blatant effort to quash the movement, petitioned the local government to investigate. They agreed.

"We cannot let this investigation move forward," Catherine said, rotating the ring around her pinky. "It will expose our complicity."

"Then we have no choice, Madame," Hugo said. "Your plan must be executed quickly. It is the only way to return peace."

"It's risky, but I agree. Arrange the meeting. Leave it to me to obtain the king's blessing."

"Yes, Madame."

Catherine met with her Italian advisors that evening at the Tuileries Palace on August 23, 1572, the eve of the Feast of Bartholomew honoring the apostle of Jesus Christ. Much later that night, she brought the scheme before the king. He reluctantly approved it at her insistence.

The queen was asleep as the sun peeked over the horizon the next morning. She awakened when Saint-Germain-l'Auxerrois's bell pierced the silence. It was the signal she had arranged for the Paris municipality to begin its slaughter of the Huguenots, starting with their nobility.

Catherine knew Admiral Coligny would be among the first killed. Still healing, he was pulled from bed and tossed out of a window. After that, the killing became indiscriminate. The Swiss Guard had already armed residents and closed the city gates so the Protestants could not escape. She had directed for their homes and shops to be plundered. Families were murdered while they slept, including women and children. Bodies piled up in the streets. They were loaded into carts and dumped into the

Seine. From her window, Catherine watched the river run red with blood.

The carnage spread into the provinces throughout the day and into more cities across France. When it subsided three weeks later, as many as ten thousand Huguenots had been killed in Paris and the provinces. Henry of Navaree, Catherine's son-in-law, barely escaped by convincing his captors he would convert to Catholicism. Once free and out of France, he renounced his conversion.

To establish the "official version" of events, Catherine advised the king to admit to ordering the massacre to foil a plot against the royal family. A jubilee, including a procession, celebrated the failure of the attempted coup. Meanwhile, the killings continued. Instead of ending religious differences, the butchery reinforced Huguenot conviction that Catholicism was a treacherous ruling influence.

"The king is mad, I tell you, mad!" Catherine shouted. She spun her sapphire ring so furiously around her finger that it flew off her hand. It bounced along the wooden floor and underneath a heavy ornate mahogany cabinet, where it fell through a gap in the floorboards.

"Your ring!" Hugo rushed over to see if he could recover it.

"Leave it!" Catherine ordered. "We have more important issues to attend to, like the king's lunacy."

"Surely you jest, Madame."

Catherine paced the room in step to the rapid thumping of her heart. "All he does is hold his ears and declares he hears the screams of the murdered Huguenots. He cries out, 'What bloodshed! What murders! What evil counsel I have followed! Oh my God, forgive me! I am lost, I am lost!' He has lost his mind, I tell you!"

The queen wrung her hands as though it would purge her of responsibility.

"I'm sure it will subside," Hugo said. "Give him time."

But neither time, nor lighted candles, nor Catherine's prayerful petitions healed the king's mind. His body began to fail as well. Coughing fits led to throwing up blood. Catherine was devastated when her third son died May 30, 1574, at age twenty-four.

Once again in a place of power, Catherine ordered Count Montgomery beheaded to exact revenge for her son's and husband's deaths, both of which she blamed on the Count and his newly found religion. Shortly thereafter, her fourth and favorite son, Henry, twenty-three, became king. His reign would be riddled with enduring warfare between Catholics and Protestants.

During this time, Hugo died and Catherine forgot about the ring. It remained lodged beneath the floorboards upon her death from pneumonia in January 1589 at age seventy.

Father Albert left an epilog at the end of the chapter:

Catherine's death was timely. Had she lived six months longer her heart would have been pierced to the core by an invisible dagger when Henry died as a result of a Dominican friar stabbing him to death. His murder was in retaliation for the king's ordering the death of the Duke of Guise and his brother, a cardinal. Both were popular figures within France's Catholic citizenry.

~~~

Abel closed the book and rubbed his weary eyes with his knuckles. While he was familiar with the names Martin Luther and John Calvin and their association with the protestant movement, he had no idea of the intense persecution their undertaking had endured. Nor had he realized the amount of power Catherine de' Medici had wielded or the depth of her involvement in the persecution of the Huguenots.

When the fire faded out to nothing more than red embers, Able selected three logs from a nearby stack and placed them onto the coals. In seconds, a blaze of renewed vigor lit up his face. The door opened as Abel turned around, and Father Albert peeked into the room.

"Ah, I see you've managed not to fall asleep." He crossed the room.

"It would have been difficult to sleep through that chapter." Abel sighed.

"Hungry?"

"Famished."

"Breakfast will be served in the kitchen. Please join me."

Abel placed *The Women of the Ring* on the side table and followed the priest.

Chapter 7

Julia opened her eyes and twisted her wrist to look at her Fitbit: 9:00 a.m. Sunday. Time to work out.

She slipped into shorts and a sleeveless T-shirt and turned on her NordicTrack looming in a corner of her living room. Although the machine hogged considerable space in her compact, contemporary one-bedroom apartment, she still had room for the essentials – a sectional couch, side chair, coffee table and storage cabinets. The TV was mounted on the wall, though with the demands of her job, she rarely had time to watch it or a Netflix movie except on weekends.

As she ran, she thought about Mr. Moody. Yep, she would call the police if she didn't hear from him by tomorrow. Probably not much they could do, but she wanted to make sure he wasn't lying on the floor of his apartment all alone. She wouldn't be able to forgive herself if no one checked.

In the meantime, she would make her weekly visit that night to her grandmother in the nursing home and ask her more about the ring. Although dementia patients struggled with their short-term memory, their long-term memory was stronger and recalled childhood songs and experiences. Her grandmother was only nine when Louise died, so perhaps she could remember something — anything — about the ring's history.

The forty-five minute drive took Julia to The Forum, a facility for patients with dementia. She stopped at the nurse's station on the fourth floor.

"How is she today?"

"Happy as a lark," Serena said. "Sometimes seniors with dementia get belligerent, but not your grandma. She may not know where she is or even who she is, but she's happy. A real blessing."

"Yes, I'm grateful for that. Well, I think I'll take her down for dinner now."

"She'll enjoy that."

Julia entered through the open door of her grandmother's cozy room, which consisted of a small sitting area, bed with dresser, and bathroom. She found her grandmother sitting in her recliner in front of the TV with Spanish dialogue flowing from the channel.

"Hi, Grandma." Julia grinned as she switched off the TV and the foreign language her seventy-seven-year-old grandmother didn't understand.

"Hi, dear." Frances's silver hair was brushed back from her blanched oval face that had just a hint of pink blush on the cheeks. A printed blouse of red, yellow, and purple garden flowers on a white background hung loosely over beige slacks. She looked up and grinned broadly. "Who are you?"

Julia planted a kiss on her wrinkled cheek. "I'm Julia, your granddaughter, and I'm going to take you down to dinner. How does that sound?"

"Well, that's nice, dear." Frances walked obediently toward the door. "I hope they have mashed potatoes tonight."

The two women walked hand in hand to the elevator. After a dinner of meatloaf, mashed potatoes, green beans, and apple pie Julia escorted Frances back up to the apartment and settled her into her recliner. The chair, covered in deep red leather, France's favorite color, had been a gift from Julia's mother when she moved into the nursing home.

"Grandmother, I want to show you something." Julia withdrew a sheet of paper from her bag. She had taken a photo of the blue sapphire ring before turning it over to Abel and printed an enlargement on her inkjet printer. She knelt beside Frances's chair and held the image in front of her. "Do you remember this ring? You gave it to me seven years ago. I was to use it for my engagement when I decided to marry."

Frances smiled and looked at the photo. Her hazel eyes revealed no recognition, but then they grew wide. She took the paper from Julia and laid it in her lap. Her long, thin fingers stroked the image as if memories radiated from it. Her smile began to fade, and her chin quivered.

"Louise."

"That's right, grandmother. This is Louise's ring. Do you remember Louise?" Julia searched her grandmother's face with eager eyes.

Frances lifted her head and glanced across the room with a faraway look. She slapped at the photo. "She was murdered!"

"Do you remember Vera, your aunt?"

"Vera? Yes. Dear Vera. She gave me the ring." Again, Frances stroked the image.

"Grandmother, now this is important: Do you know how Louise got the ring?"

Frances turned to her granddaughter, expressionless. Without a word, she rose and walked across the room to her dresser. Julia followed. What was she doing?

Frances opened the top drawer and reached beneath her under clothes. She withdrew a paperback book and handed it to Julia.

"It's all there." Frances tapped the well-worn book with her index finger.

The title was imprinted in red on a black cover — *Who Killed Leno and Louise?*. The cover was creased, and some of the pages were dog-eared. Gee, how many times had it been read? Hundreds? Julia didn't even know a book existed on the seventy-year-old murders.

"Thank you, grandma, thank you." Julia gave her grandmother a big hug and Julia settled her back into the recliner. "Grandma, do you remember when you found out about Louise and Leno being murdered?"

Tears welled in Frances's eyes as she looked at Julia. "An awful day. We were just coming back from church. I was eight and skipping up the sidewalk to my grandmother's house. We always had Sunday dinner there with the rest of the family. We hadn't even gotten into the door when Aunt Vera screamed that Leno and Louise had been murdered. Nobody knew why. All the adults were crying and went into the den to talk about it. I guess they forgot about me. I stood in the foyer feeling cold, like I had no blood. Why would someone want to kill Leno and Louise?"

Julia patted her grandmother's hand. "Don't worry, grandma, I'll keep the book safe and bring it back when I'm finished. See you next week." She kissed her grandmother on the cheek. "I love you."

Frances smiled at Julia. "What's your name, dear?"

That night, Julia snuggled into bed with the book. She propped her back against the headboard and opened the cover. A newspaper correspondent, Sarah Landers, had written it. Once Julia began reading, she couldn't put it down. The murders were part of her family history that she had heard only snippets about from her aunts and uncles. No one had wanted to talk about the stinging event, so she never knew the whole story. Now she had an opportunity to learn more about Leno and Louise and why they were murdered. She knew the ring had played a key role, but why?

When Julia awoke in the morning at 6:30 a.m., the book was open beside her. Oh, the bed felt so good. She just wanted to curl up to finish the book, but she had to get to work. Hmm . . . . she hadn't used any of her personal days.

She phoned her assistant and let her know she would not be in. Then she brewed some coffee and toasted an English muffin. She took them back to the room with her and settled into bed to disappear into the book.

Her cell phone rang. Noon? She was still in her pajamas!

"Hey, I called your office and they said you were taking a personal day. Are you all right?" Winston's tone exuded concern.

"Oh, I'm fine. My grandmother gave me a book about Leno and Louise's murders, so I thought I'd take a day off to read it. Fascinating stuff."

"Want to tell me about it over dinner?"

"Would love to. How about we meet at Chalky's at seven for a drink, then go to Sal's for their lasagna special?"

"Perfect, see you then."

Julia spent the day finishing the book. In the evening, she took a shower and dressed for her dinner date with Winston. They entered Chalky's and found its typically noisy crowd along with several patrons engaged in an impassioned game of darts. They ordered glasses of Sauvignon blanc at the bar and scanned the room, hoping someone would vacate a booth.

"We got a big client today," Winston said.

"Another one? That's the fourth in two weeks. Your little IT company isn't so little anymore. I'm so proud of you." Julia kissed Winston's cheek.

"It's the sales force. They're really good. I guess a better than average commission along with a salary doesn't hurt either." Winston smiled and took a sip of his wine.

"Oh look, that couple is leaving." Julia tossed her head toward a corner booth, and she and Winston rushed over to it.

"So, what's up with the book?" Winston asked over the din of '70s music, conversations, and laughter.

"Well, Leno and Louise were quite the couple. I knew he was an Italian artist — sculptures, bas-reliefs, statues, and the like — but I never knew how accomplished Louise was. And the ring? Well, that goes back to the late 1930s. At least, that's the earliest information about it, according to the book."

"Is that when Louise got it?"

"Yes, Grandmother was right when she remembered Louise's employer, Dolly O'Brien, gave her the ring. Now there's one fascinating woman!"

"You're losing me. How about starting at the beginning?"

"Okay." Julia sipped her wine and folded her arms on the table. "It begins with Dolly. She was born into wealth and high society in Connecticut. She married her first husband, Louis Marshall Heminway, at fifteen, but he died only three years later and left her very wealthy with two young sons. Enter Julius Fleischmann of the Fleischmann's

Yeast empire. He was twenty years older than Dolly, but that didn't seem to matter. He saw the young, beautiful widow and proposed, even though he knew she didn't love him. She accepted and moved into his posh Long Island estate with her sons.

"He was an accomplished polo player who hosted players at the estate during polo season. One of them was James Jay 'J.J.' O'Brien. He put the moves on Dolly, and the two fell in love. Dolly divorced Julius, settled for interest in the Cincinnati Reds baseball team and several million of his fifty million dollar estate, and married J.J. in 1924. They moved into a grand estate down in Palm Beach, Florida." Julia paused for a sip of wine.

Winston drummed his fingers on the table. "I thought this story was about the ring."

"It is, but you can't rush a good story." Julia laughed and took another sip. "Dolly went with J.J. to New York City for a speaking engagement he had. At their hotel, Dolly used Louise, the hotel's on-call stenographer, to dictate letters. She liked Louise so much that she hired her as her private assistant and took her back to Palm Beach. Louise worked for Dolly for six years and became the manager of J.J.'s West Palm Beach radio station WKNO. It was at one of Palm Beach's upper-crust cultural events that she met Leno Lazzari, an Italian sculptor. He had a studio on Via Parizi on Worth Avenue, a posh shopping venue in Palm Beach. They fell in love and got married. She and Leno lived in West Palm Beach, so Louise continued to work for Dolly.

"Leno had some property in Boca Raton and decided to build an apartment and studio there. During its construction, Louise turned in her notice to Dolly because the drive would be too far every day. Now here's where the ring comes in. Are you ready?"

Winston sat up straight and gestured "bring it on" with his hands.

"Dolly wanted to reward Louise for her faithful service, so Dolly gave her a ring. She told Louise she bought it in Paris. Winston . . . it's our ring — the one we're using for our engagement!"

Winston's brown eyes widened, and his forehead crinkled. "So our ring came from Paris?"

"Yes, but there's much, much more. Louise wore the ring on special occasions and kept it and other pieces in a small jewelry box in the center drawer of her wooden desk. The night she and Leno were murdered, her jewelry was stolen to make it look like a robbery. Palm Beach County deputies took everything from the studio back to the sheriff's office and looked through it for evidence. Two days later, the jewelry box magically reappeared back in the desk with the ring and other pieces.

"The sheriff's office never followed the trail of the jewelry box's disappearance and astounding return. Instead, they went on some wild goose chase after a man who abandoned a car about a mile from the studio the night of the murders. The murders were never solved and remain a cold case. Louise's sister, Vera, inherited the ring, and gave it to my grandmother." Julia crossed her arms and sat back.

Winston drained his glass and appeared deep in thought. He leaned his tall frame over the table.

"Babe, are you sure you want to wear a ring that's tied to such a sad and tragic event?"

Julia stiffened. "I guess I never thought of it like that. I always looked at is as a way to honor the women in my family."

Winston tilted his head and raised one eyebrow in a questionable expression.

Julia grabbed her wrap. "Ready for dinner?"

Chapter 8

Abel stepped into the modest kitchen in the back of the church and sat at an old wooden table inlaid with decorative tile — hand-painted grapes, watermelons, apples, corn, tomatoes, and beans on a white glossy background — much like one would find in a farmhouse.

"No one to cook for you?" Abel watched Father Albert scramble four eggs and place half alongside three sausage links on each plate, which was loaded with tomato slices, wedges of Camembert cheese, and slices of crusty French bread.

"This is her day off. That's when I do the cooking. And to honor my guest, I made an American meal." Father Albert joined Abel at the table and blessed the food.

"Funny, isn't it? Here we are, a Catholic and a Protestant sitting down together to enjoy a meal and conversation. That wouldn't have happened in Catherine de'

Medici's time." Abel buttered his bread and topped it with cheese.

"Thankfully, we've come a long way since then." Father Albert shook salt and pepper on his eggs.

"Amen. Strange to think the early church evolved into that. I don't think Christ planned it that way."

"It is unfortunate man's pride and thirst for power morphed into such an unchristian attitude."

They finished their meal in silence.

Father Albert gathered the dishes. "Would you like to sleep a bit before you get into the next chapter? There's a bed in the guest room. You're welcome to use it."

"Perhaps for a few hours. I don't want to overstay my welcome."

"Nonsense. You're here to read the book so you can understand why our task is so important. I didn't expect you to finish it in one sitting. Besides, we can't complete our mission for several days."

"In that case, I accept."

Father Albert led Abel to a comfortable room with a single bed with fresh linens, a small table, and a plain wooden chair. The bathroom was down the hall. Abel slipped off his loafers and lay on the bed. He hoped to ponder what he had read, but he quickly fell into a coma-like sleep.

Five hours later, he awoke and returned to the library.

~~~

Francesca Grimaldi

It was past midnight. The kitchen staff had retired to bed, all except Francesca Grimaldi.

Standing on a footstool, her four-foot-ten-inch frame hunched over the sink in the scullery, arms elbow deep in soapsuds, where she scoured the last copper pot from dinner with a fine scrubber until it shined.

As the newest scullery maid at the palace, it was her job to perform the final cleanup after dinner. At fourteen, she had arrived at the Vincennes palace in the heart of Paris three months earlier on the recommendation of a distant cousin who worked in the stable. It was a position her mother prayed she would get because income from their small family farm had plummeted since her father recently had died of a heart attack.

While she hated leaving her mother alone on the farm and friends behind in the village, she would have this job well into adulthood if it worked out. Thankfully, her expenses were minimal because the palace provided most of her room and board. This allowed her to send a substantial amount of her salary home to her mother. Being a scullery maid certainly wasn't the future she envisioned, but she could survive, and she could move up in rank if they liked her and she did a good job. Right now, though, she had to fulfill her obligation.

Francesca brushed a blond wisp of hair from her face to the back of her ear. Standing in the center of the room wearing a beige muslin dress overlaid with a pink apron, she smiled as her eyes swept the room. The scullery was spotless with every pot and pan washed, dried, and stored away. She took pride in her work even though she had one of the lowliest jobs at the palace.

Finally, bedtime.

She lifted a small lantern from its hook to light the way to her sleeping quarters. As she crossed the room, she tilted her head back to stretch her neck. That's when she saw it – a glint from the ceiling boards. It vanished the moment she moved. She shifted back and raised the lantern over her head. There it was again. A twinkle.

Francesca carried a heavy wooden chair from the staff's dining table and positioned it under the sparkle. She stepped onto the seat and raised the lantern again, but she wasn't high enough to determine the source. If she stepped onto the cupboard shelf from the chair, however, she would be directly under it.

With caution, she placed her foot onto the shelf and shifted her weight until she was standing on the cupboard. She raised the lantern and could see the glimmer quite clearly. Something blue, but she needed a tool — a thin object to stick between the ceiling slats so she could manipulate the object.

She selected a paring knife from the drawer and climbed back onto the cupboard. Setting the lantern on top to free her hands, she slid the blade between the boards and wriggled it against the object until she recognized it — a ring with a blue stone. How beautiful! How did it get there? More importantly, how to get it out?

Her eyes followed the ceiling boards to the wall. They joined at the corner in a wider gap. Maybe she could push the ring to that spot and chip a bit of wood from the ceiling board.

Francesca coaxed the ring across the ceiling. When it was close to the junction, she inserted the knife tip and carefully removed tiny pieces of wood until the cavity in the corner was large enough for the ring to fall through.

Just as it landed in her hand, the door to the scullery opened.

Rupert, valet to Philippe, Le Duc d'Orleans, stood in the doorway in his black-and-white uniform, hands on his hips. "What are you doing up there?" He never went to bed before the duke.

Startled, Francesca almost lost her footing, but managed to catch herself by jumping onto the chair. She whisked the ring into her skirt pocket.

"Cleaning the top of the cupboard." She knew who Rupert was, but the two had never spoken. She cast her eyes downward as pink splotches bloomed on her neck and face.

"With that?" Rupert pointed at the knife in her hand.

"It gets into all the little crevasses." She twisted the steel blade so the light reflected off of it. Did that sound believable?

"Well, the duke wants something to eat."

Francesca looked around. "All the kitchen staff has gone to bed. I'm the only one here."

"You'll do. Bring him some bread and a bowl of tonight's soup."

"But, won't you take it to him?"

Francesca had been told in her orientation that everyone had to follow certain protocols for their specific job. Her job was relegated to the bowel of the castle. She was never to venture out of it except in her free time — and only out the back door.

"He's in the library. You *do* know where that is, don't you?"

Francesca had been given a tour of the main floor and its rooms but had only been upstairs once since then. Fortunately, it had been to the library.

"Yes, I know where it is. Please tell the duke I'll have his food soon. I just need to warm the soup."

"Very well, but don't take too long."

Francesca knew this request was highly unusual. A lowly scullery maid never went upstairs or brought food to members of the French court, but what could she do? She didn't want to seem insubordinate and get fired after just three months, so she laid a log on the embers in the stove so she could heat up the soup and scurried around the kitchen trying to find all the items she needed. She warmed the chicken soup in a pot, cut a thick slice of brown bread from the loaf, poured a glass of cabernet, and set the tray with a fresh white linen napkin. She even pulled a daisy from the bouquet on the staff dining table for a garnish.

Just as she was about to ascend the stairs to the main level, she caught a glimpse of herself in the round wall mirror. Her white cap was askew, and blond hair poked out in all directions. She put the tray down and pushed the unruly strands back under her cap and straightened it. At least her face was clean and her blue eyes bright. But her hands were rough — red and chapped from all day in soapy water. Thankfully, the duke would be looking at her face and not her hands, but her soiled apron was a disgrace! She pulled it off and tossed it over the railing.

Francesca climbed the stairs one at a time, careful not to spill anything. Her knees quivered causing the wine glass to clink against the soup bowl. At the library, she balanced the tray on her knee and knocked on the door.

"Enter!" the duke said.

Francesca opened the eight-foot-tall, elaborately carved door and curtsied in the entry. "Your soup, sir."

"Close the door and bring it here."

She noticed the duke surveying her youthful figure from his red-and-gold brocade couch as she walked across the room. His heart-shaped effeminate face was accented by a black goatee and a handlebar mustache that curled up at the ends. Dark brows arched over obsidian eyes, and his black hair draped well past his shoulders and down his back in a multitude of waves. He motioned for Francesca to place the tray on a small table inlayed with mother of pearl flowers in front of him.

"Is that all, sir?" Without the tray, Francesca felt naked in front of the duke, who appeared to be about ten years older than her.

"Perhaps not. Remove your cap." He sat back and with a wry grin spread his arms along the top of the couch.

"My cap?"

"Yes, and undo your hair." Philippe's eyes glowed in the dim light as he licked his lips.

"Sir, I must go. I need to finish cleaning the kitchen." Francesca rushed toward the door and felt the ornate doorknob in her hand just as the duke stabbed her with his stern voice.

"You do wish to retain your job, don't you?"

Francesca froze.

"Of course, sir," she said in a trembling voice. She turned around slowly.

"Then . . ." Philippe splayed his hands.

Francesca's quaking fingers untied her cap and stuffed it into her pocket. Adrenaline shot through her like a bolt of lightning as she felt the ring. If the duke found that, she would be accused of stealing and thrown out of the palace! Her reputation would be ruined, and she'd never get another job. She felt like a fly stuck to sticky paper.

"Yes, now undo your hair." The duke straightened and studied her as she released her golden locks to cascade over her shoulders.

"Beautiful," he said in a lustful tone. "Now come here."

Francesca wobbled as she walked slowly toward him.

"Sit down." Philippe patted the cushion next to him.

The scent of the duke's cologne, a mixture of leather and spiced liqueur, swelled in Francesca's nostrils as she sat on the couch. The duke stroked her hair and nuzzled her ear.

"Everyone's fast asleep," he whispered. "Besides, do you think anyone would dare interrupt us?"

Francesca's eyes grew wide and terror gripped her as she felt herself being lowered onto the couch and the duke's hand beneath her skirt.

Days dragged by. Francesca faced each night with trepidation, dreading a summons from the duke. After several weeks, she relaxed and enjoyed a picnic down by the river with other staff on her day off, stiffening only when someone mentioned the duke's name.

She slept in every morning until nine because she worked the afternoon shift from 3:00 p.m. to midnight. Occasionally, she had to help during the day when there was a special event, such as the queen's luncheon or a meeting of the French court. Her days proved very long when that happened, but it all seemed worthwhile when she received her pay at the end of the month.

Everything seemed back to normal until the day she could hardly get out of bed because she was so nauseous. Though she tried to work, the task of cleaning food from plates sent her scurrying to the bathroom. After eight days of this, she was fired and returned home to her mother.

Back home on the farm, speculation grew among neighbors as to why she had been let go. Francesca insisted she had a stomach ailment, but she knew her deception had much more to do with her swelling breasts. She stayed indoors except when needed to help her mother milk the cows or tend the pigs. When feeling up to it, she'd walked a mile to the river through the forest of tall elm trees. She loved their stately trunks and the sway of their boughs when the wind blew through them. At the river, she often lingered on the bridge and stared down into the swift current. Oh, how she wished she could float out to sea on it and away from her shame!

Francesca's nausea subsided as her belly began to show. She knew it would only be a matter of time before her mother noticed. That morning came all too soon.

"Who is he? Who is the father of this bastard child?" Carmen stood by her daughter's bed, arms crossed in front of her. She had held her daughter's heaving body innumerable times while she threw up into a bucket, now she wanted some answers. "I sent you to work, but apparently you had other ideas. How could you?"

Tears slid down Francesca's face as she sat up in bed and tried not to break down. "You won't believe me. Nobody would."

Her mother shook her daughter's shoulders. "I want the truth!"

"It's the duke's child!" Francesca wailed. "He forced himself on me months ago. I never told anyone."

Her mother jerked back in surprise. "The duke?"

"Yes, Philippe. Le Duc d'Orleans. The king's son." Francesca told her the whole sordid story through sobs. "And here . . . here's the ring that kept me in the scullery late that night." She crossed the room in a huff and retrieved it from her dresser. "None of this would have happened if I had gone to bed instead of trying to pry it from the ceiling." She slapped the ring into the hand of her mother, who studied it.

"Why, this is worth a fortune, Francesca! We can sell it and live quite comfortably."

Francesca drew her sleeved arm across her runny nose. "We can't sell the ring, Mother. Who would buy it from us? Who would believe we simply found it? I don't know whose it is, but we would both be thrown into jail if word of this ever got back to the duke! No, the ring is just as cursed as I am." Francesca threw herself onto her pillow and sobbed uncontrollably.

"Shush, my child." Her mother rubbed her back with a soothing touch. "I'll think of something."

The closer Francesca drew to delivery, the more desperate she and her mother became. They could probably hide her pregnancy, but who would deliver the baby? Even if they swore a midwife to secrecy, how would she conceal a baby's cry or growing child? They couldn't hide it in the house forever. They could lie, of course, and say the baby belonged to a relative who couldn't take care of it. But everyone in the village knew their family, their history. It appeared the window God promised would open whenever a door closed was nailed shut.

Francesca was peeling potatoes over the sink when her water broke and the searing pains erupted. Carmen, who was outside feeding the pigs, rushed inside when she heard the screams. Francesca was panting and gritting her teeth on the wooden floor. Sweat glistened on her face, and water puddled on the floor. She watched her mother rush upstairs to fetch clean towels and sheets before putting a pot of water on the stove to boil.

Six long hours later, Francesca pushed for the last time. She delivered a baby girl.

Two days later, Francesca peered out the upstairs window and watched her mother hitch their horse to the wagon and head into the village for supplies. Once she was out of sight, Francesca swaddled the sleeping baby in a blanket and tucked her into a large reed basket, like one would carry on a picnic. She covered it with a thin tablecloth and headed for the river.

When she got to the pasture thick with summer grasses, she turned and took one last gaze at the farm before opening the gate and crossing the field where a dozen cattle grazed. She reached the river twenty minutes later. Under a wide oak surrounded by tall reeds, she spread the tablecloth on the ground and placed the basket on it. The baby was still sleeping.

Francesca looked down at the peaceful infant and smiled. Such a beautiful child, yet the shame she would cause them was immeasurable. Her smile crumbled to tears. She knelt down and kissed the baby tenderly on the forehead.

As she walked to the river's edge, she noticed a lone fisherman tossing his line into the water some distance away. She had seen him before around this time of day. He seemed quite content in the bright sunshine awaiting a bite.

Her first step into the water sent a shiver up her spine as the cool water swirled around her ankle.

She took another step.

Then another.

She waded farther and farther from the bank until the swift current swept her off her feet. She heard the baby cry just as the water was about to swallow her. Oh, how she wanted to turn back, but it was too late. She trusted God that the fisherman would hear her baby's cry.

~~~

Abel looked up from his reading. To think the young girl felt she had no way out broke his heart. What happened to the baby? And, what happened to the ring? He felt sure the next chapter would explain it.

The clock chimed 11:30 a.m. All he'd done the past two days was read, eat, and sleep, but he had to finish the book. He needed to understand the entire story if he and Father Albert were going to follow through with their plan,

Abel rose and stretched his stiff limbs. He craved a shower, shave, and change of clothes. He also needed some fresh air. He searched for Father Albert, but unable to find him he left a note on his chair that he was going back to the hotel and would return later that evening.

He opened the wooden door through which he had first entered and inhaled a deep breath of the brisk Paris air. It smelled clean, not dank like it did when the fog shrouded the city and soot from fires infused every breath. The sun hid behind a layer of high, thin clouds, punctuated by periodic brushes of robin's egg blue. Branches from the trees, still bare from winter, appeared like dark tendrils against the sky as though pleading for God to touch them with his palette of spring green.

Abel zipped up his jacket and wandered down the brick walkway through the headstones toward the street. The cemetery in the daylight was far less intimidating than in the foggy gloom of night. Now he could see the dates of the deceased — 1856, 1799, 1702 — and the names of Rob Corner, Phoenicia Henry, and Jaco Bellemare. Who were they? What had their lives been like? What had they done for a living? How had they died?

Rounding a corner, Able noticed an empty space between two headstones. When he stepped closer, though, he saw a simple rectangular stone mounted flush to the ground, unlike the other graves with vertical headstones. A jagged crack from a tree root meandered through the surface, and a morning glory vine with pink blossoms crawled over the pitted, weathered face, obscuring the deceased's name. Only the first two numbers of the year of death peeked through: 16--. This was the earliest marker he had seen. Whose was it? He untangled the vine with the end of his cane, and a chill coursed through him as he read the inscription: Francesca Grimaldi, 1650-1665.

Discovering her grave and childhood parish was most unexpected, but it didn't divulge the whole story. He didn't see a grave for the baby. What had happened to her?

That Father Albert may have uncovered Francesca's story in the pages of the library books was certainly plausible. Churches historically kept detailed records of the births, marriages, and deaths of its parish members. In fact, Francesca Grimaldi's life was probably just one of hundreds of long-forgotten histories documented in the books lining the library shelves.

Finding Francesca's grave right after reading her story seemed a highly unusual coincidence. Yet how many more lay ahead involving the ring?

Chapter 9

It was past 7:00 p.m. on Monday when Winston pulled his BMW into a parking space at the 62nd Precinct in Brooklyn. Street lamps illuminated the three-story building at the corner of Bath Avenue and Bay 22nd Street. The first floor's light-gray block served as foundation for the red brick on the upper two floors. Ornate corbels accented a green roof, and round and rectangular medallions decorated the side of the building. Air-conditioner units protruded from a multitude of windows like dark appendages.

Julia took a deep breath. She had never been to a police station and wished she didn't have to visit this one. The imposing building and half a dozen police vehicles was intimidating enough, but then a uniformed officer guided a young man in handcuffs past them and up the front steps into the building.

"Are you sure you want to do this ?" Winston said.

"Of course," Julia said, trying to hide her nerves. "We have to make sure Mr. Moody is all right, don't we?" Julia swallowed and opened the car door.

Inside, they passed through a foyer with chairs and approached a glass window similar to the ones in medical offices with one exception — this one didn't slide open. Round glass at head height with a multitude of drilled holes allowed conversation while a slot at the bottom could accept paperwork. Behind the glass, which Julia assumed was bulletproof, sat a uniformed female officer with the name Perez on her badge.

"May I help you?" she asked. She looked from Winston to Julia.

"We'd like to speak with someone regarding . . ." Julia's chin quivered and her eyes teared as she looked at Winston and back at the officer.

Winston pulled Julia close. "Officer, we'd like to report someone missing."

"May I see your IDs?"

They slid their driver's licenses through the slot to Officer Perez. She scanned them and handed them back. "Have a seat. Someone will be right with you."

After a few minutes, an officer introduced himself as Sergeant Earnest and escorted them through a secure door into a room jammed with cubicles. The muffled sound of ringing phones, conversations, and clicking computer keys rose above the semi-private partitions and merged in a cacophony of muted noise. Winston and Julia followed the sergeant to a small room with a table, three chairs, and a glass window reinforced with chicken wire that looked out onto the street. Julia surmised the room was used for interrogations.

"Please sit down and tell me about this missing person." The sergeant placed his laptop on the table, swiped at the screen, and poised his hands over the keys ready to take notes.

"Well, we're not sure he's missing," Julia said. "It's just that we haven't heard from him in days despite repeated attempts to contact him. He's elderly and lives alone. We just thought maybe you should check to make sure nothing has happened to him."

"Let's start with his name first and your relationship to him." Sergeant Earnest took down all the particulars regarding Mr. Moody: name, address, name of the shop, phone number, age, how Julia knew him, and the date Julia concluded he was missing.

Julia related how he had oddly questioned the history of the ring after she delivered it to him and that he closed the shop soon after. She added that no one had heard from him since.

"Would there be any reason for him to take the ring?" Sergeant Earnest asked.

Julia's eyes grew wide at the officer. "You mean steal it? Why, I'd never even considered that possibility! I've known Mr. Moody since I was a child. He's the most honest person I know. Besides, he's got all kinds of jewelry in his cases. Why would he want my ring?"

"I don't know, ma'am, but it's my job to consider all the possibilities. Could you please describe the ring?"

Julia gave him a copy of the image she had printed out. "Can you help us?"

"We'll do our best, ma'am. And thank you for coming in. It was the right thing to do. Can't tell you how many elderly folks we find who don't have anyone to be concerned about them. We'll check out the premises, canvass the neighbors again, and call the alarm company in case they know something. We'll get back to you with an update. Again, thank you for coming in."

Julia went to work Wednesday, but had difficulty concentrating. She was anxious to hear from Sergeant Earnest and still hadn't heard anything by the time she left the office. She was driving home in her car when her cell rang, and she answered through Bluetooth.

"Hi, sergeant. I've been waiting to hear from you. Any news about Mr. Moody?"

"Yes and no. We checked out his store, and like you said, it's closed tight with the security gate down. The alarm company hasn't heard from him and actually was wondering about him themselves because he hasn't been in the store since he set the alarm last week. They said that is most unusual and have been trying to reach him. The folks in the neighboring stores still haven't heard from him either. But the good news is that your ring hasn't shown up at the local pawnshops. We'll check on a few more things and get back to you when we have some answers."

"What kind of things?"

"I'm not at liberty to divulge that right now, but I promise I'll be in touch."

That night, Julia fixed a Caesar salad with shrimp for her and Winston at her apartment. Then they settled in for a movie, something that would distract her. They settled on *The Notebook*. Julia had seen it twice before, but it was one of her favorites.

As the closing credits rolled two hours later, tears streaked her face. "Could you hand me a tissue? Even though I know the ending by heart, it always gets me. Probably not the best choice, given my mood."

"You're such a softy." Winston handed her a Kleenex box. "But I can understand why it touches you since your grandmother has dementia as well."

"Actually, it reminds me of one of the lessons Mr. Moody taught me."

"What about?"

"Love."

***

1998, Moody Jewelry & Repair

Mr. Moody sat at his long workbench repairing three watches while Julia, twelve, wiggled next to him on a swivel stool. Her notebook was open on the bench, and she flicked a pencil between her index and middle finger as she did her homework.

"Mr. Moody, how come you don't have any kids?"

He lifted his head from his work with a look of surprise. "Well, Mrs. Moody and I weren't able to have children. We tried for a long time, but she never got pregnant."

"But you love children. Why didn't you adopt?" Julia's eyes remained on her notebook, as though the question was so personal she could only hear the answer without looking at Mr. Moody.

"We thought about it, but Mrs. Moody wanted to keep trying to have children of our own."

"You must have tried a long time."

"We did. For twenty years. Eventually so much time passed that Mrs. Moody got older, and well, she just felt it was too late to have children." Mr. Moody changed out a small screwdriver for a polishing cloth.

"Did you get mad at Mrs. Moody for waiting so long?"

Mr. Moody's hands froze, and he cocked his head in thought. "I guess I did at first, but then I had to remember why I married her."

"Because you loved her?"

"Yes, but there's more to it than just the word. Miss Julia, what do you know about love?"

Julia shrugged. "I know my momma loves me, and I love her."

"Yes, that's certainly one kind of love, between a parent and a child. But there are other kinds of love as well, such as for a friend, or a pet, or a good movie — or even pepperoni pizza." He leaned over and poked Julia in the side. "You do love pepperoni pizza, don't you?"

Julia scrunched her body and laughed. "Yes, I love pepperoni pizza."

"Well, the kind of love I feel for Mrs. Moody is even better than that — deeper."

Julia's smile crashed into a frown. "I thought my father loved my mother like that, but he didn't. I guess that's why he left."

"I'm very sorry that happened. It shouldn't have. You see, love isn't a feeling like most people think. Love is a choice — and a commitment."

Julia stopped writing and swiveled to face Mr. Moody. "I don't understand."

"People say they fall in love. But, Miss Julia, love isn't something you *fall* into, like a swimming pool. It's something you *grow* into," he said, spreading his hands. "It takes time to know someone and to discover all the things you like about them and all the things you don't. Many times, finding out what you don't like about them is far more important than the things you like. I know it seems the opposite of what you'd expect."

"But won't that make you not love them anymore?"

"Well, you do have to weigh those things very carefully before you decide to marry someone. If the negatives outweigh the positives, then maybe that person just isn't right for you. But if you decide to get married, you must accept the negatives with the positives. It all goes back to love being a choice. For instance, are there some things you don't like about your mother?"

"Sure." Julia rolled her eyes. "Like the way she clinks her spoon against the side of her soup bowl. It drives me crazy."

"But do you stop loving her because of that?"

"No . . . but I wish she'd find another way to eat her soup."

"Okay, but the point is she has habits you don't like. I'm sure you do things that annoy her too. Can you think of one?"

Julia sighed and dropped her shoulders. "Not putting my clothes away."

"Great example! But your mom still loves you, doesn't she?"

"I guess."

"Well, that's the way it is supposed to be with marriage, too. Husbands and wives have things they don't like about each other, annoying things, but they make a choice to love each other despite that. They have to learn how to talk about those things so they don't become a wall between them, even if it means they agree to disagree. That's what love is all about. I call it the three Cs: communication, compromise, and commitment."

"So when Mrs. Moody couldn't have children you used the three Cs?"

"Yes, I did. But you must understand that sometimes one partner does most and maybe all of the compromising, depending upon the issue. But it might be the other person next time. When you love someone deeply, you have to weigh the issue against your history together and decide which is more important — the issue or the relationship. I chose Mrs. Moody."

"Aren't there some things that you would stop loving someone for?"

"Well, you may not like someone for doing things like drugs or physical abuse, stealing, or lying, and you may have to distance yourself from that person for a while or maybe even permanently, but you can still love them even though you can't live with them anymore."

"When you made your decision about Mrs. Moody, you had to change your way of thinking, didn't you? Like I did with the necklace?"

Mr. Moody's face lit up. "That's right." He thrust his fists on his hips. "Miss Julia, how did you get so smart?"

Julia laughed. "Hanging around you, Mr. Moody." She jumped off her stool and gave him a big hug.

**

Julia was reflecting on the memory she had just related to Winston when her phone rang. Sergeant Earnest. She put him on speaker so Winston could hear.

"Miss Townsend, we've done some further checking, and here's what we know so far. Mr. Moody withdrew a thousand dollars from the ATM at his bank on Thursday night and booked a one-way flight to Paris for Friday with his credit card. He checked in at the Hotel Caron. Do you know why he might have gone to Paris?"

Julia arched her brows at Winston. "I have no idea, sergeant. Could someone have forced him into it?"

"We've looked at the surveillance tapes at the bank and airport, and it seems he's the only one taking the trip, and he doesn't look distressed. In fact, he looks happy. Has he ever done anything like this before to your knowledge?"

"Not that I'm aware of, but I hadn't been in touch with Mr. Moody for a couple of years. So you think he's okay?"

"The good news is we know he's fine. It's just curious why he would take off like that, especially after you gave him your ring. And what's even more puzzling is that he didn't book a round-trip flight. All you can do now is wait until he returns or contacts you. And, please, keep us informed."

"Of course. Thank you for the update, sergeant. I'm relieved to hear he's okay."

"By the way, you may want to file charges if the ring doesn't surface by your engagement party."

Julia hung up, deep in thought. "Do you really think Mr. Moody took our ring to Paris?"

"Why would he do that? He knows we need it in a couple of weeks."

"I realize that, but the ring has a connection to Paris. That's where Dolly bought it."

"Hon, we'll just have to wait. There's nothing we can do right now."

Julia thought for a moment then jumped up.

"Yes, there is, Winston. We can go to Paris!"

Chapter 10

As Abel retraced his steps back to the hotel, he noticed a jewelry shop, Babioles et Jijoux, on a side street. He hadn't seen it before, but granted, it had been dark, foggy, and far too late for the store lights to be on. As a fellow tradesman, he decided to venture inside. Maybe he could learn something new from his Parisian colleagues and their designs.

A bell tinkled over the door as he stepped inside. It appeared to be a mom-and-pop store, much like his own. Jewelry glimmered in glass cases that formed an L against a corner. A workbench ran the length of the walls behind the cases. A man sat on a stool with his back to Abel, probably working on repairs. A middle-aged woman with short, curly brown hair smiled at Abel from behind the counter. "Bonjour."

"Bonjour, do you speak English?" Abel asked.

"Oui, we speak English here." Her friendly look turned into a stare as her eyes scanned every detail of Abel's face. "Excuse me, monsieur, I do not wish to be rude, but you seem familiar. Have we met?"

"No, I just arrived in Paris a couple of days ago. I just noticed your store and thought I'd drop in."

The woman tilted her head. "It's just that you look like someone I know."

Abel smiled. "I assure you I just arrived in your city and have never visited Paris or your store before."

"Very well, monsieur, I'm Celeste. How can I help you?"

He handed the woman one of his cards. She looked at it and then at Abel.

"Ah, Mr. Moody, I see you are a jeweler. A master jeweler perhaps?"

Abel chuckled and shook his head. "No, not a master jeweler from the view of a European. I've never served as an indentured apprentice or made a masterpiece of jewelry to present to a jury of craftsmen who would award me certification. Though the years under my father's and grandfather's tutelage could have qualified. They were masters of their craft. I learned from them."

"You must meet our master jeweler. You two have much in common."

Abel's eyes widened. "I'd love to!"

"Just one moment." Celeste's smile turned into a wry grin as though a secret lay just beyond her lips. She slipped through a door behind the counter and emerged with a black man. He appeared about the same height as Abel and wore street clothes covered by a jeweler's apron. His eyes were downturned looking at Abel's business card as he approached the counter.

"Monsieur Moody, this is Masego Bamudy," Celeste said.

She stepped aside to reveal the man behind her. When he lifted his eyes to greet Abel, he stared in surprise. Abel stared back. It was as though they were looking in a mirror — broad nose, square chin, high cheekbones, dark eyes. Masego was a reflection of a much younger version of Abel, one from thirty years ago. Both men were speechless.

"Perhaps you two should go to the café and talk?" Celeste said.

"Good idea," Masego said.

He removed his apron and exchanged it for a jacket, before leading Abel down the block and around the corner to Bien Café. They sat at an alfresco bistro table for two and ordered coffee. The sun felt warm even though the temperature was cool.

"Masego . . . I know that name," Abel said, thinking back to the *Women of the Ring*. "But from centuries ago. He was a master jeweler's apprentice right here in Paris."

"My family from Tanzania has been in Paris since the 1500s. The name Masego was passed down to the eldest boy of each generation. The Masego you mentioned was the first to make it out of Tanzania. I am the seventh generation Masego."

Abel sat in shock. Could he be looking into the eyes of a descendant of the same Masego who redesigned Mary of Burgundy's ring? And even if he was, how in the world could he and Masego resemble each other so much?

"Please, it is vitally important that I know your family history," Abel said.

"Interesting. The only other person who has asked me that was Father Albert from the church. Do you know him?"

Abel drew back. "Yes. Actually, he's why I'm in Paris. But, please, go on with the story of your family." Abel leaned in. He didn't want to miss a single word.

"My family worked in a crude gem mine in Tanzania, one of only a handful in Africa that supplied most of the gemstones for the royalty of Europe. It was a lucrative business for the mine owners, but a horrible existence for the workers. The shafts were steep and narrow. They didn't have equipment to pump fresh air into the chambers — only a makeshift bellows system. The workers dug in shifts of only thirty or maybe forty-five minutes as the carbon dioxide built up in their blood streams. They gasped for air when they came out. But the bosses sent them back down as soon as they deemed them fit. They were beaten if they couldn't work. Many died from the poisonous air, others from the beatings. Basically, the workers were expendable, much like the slaves building the pyramids of Egypt. When one man fell, many more could take his place." Masego sipped his coffee. His eyes reflected the sorrow he felt for his people.

Abel was mortified over such hardship. "Why did your family do this? Couldn't they have been farmers, or carpenters, or something else?"

"You must understand, Africa was divided into tribes, not countries like we have today, and every tribe had a territory, much like Europe. Every tribal leader wanted more land, more power. The strongest leader with the best-trained warriors proved victorious. The spoils of war were the conquered territory and the defeated people. The winner moved into the land and took the people as slaves. My people were some of them. That's how they wound up working the gem mines, because that's where the money was made to run the empire — by each cleave of a hammer and each breath of a slave. Most American blacks think Africans became slaves under white suppression, but our own people enslaved us. When America needed slaves, it was African blacks who sold their own people all over the Caribbean and Americas."

"How did Masego get out and make his way to Paris?" Abel was so mesmerized that he let his coffee turn cold.

"Most of the slaves worked the mines, but Masego proved very good at cutting the gemstones, so he worked in the factory. The gems, both raw and faceted, were sold to jewelers like Louis Van Berquem or directly to the royalty in Europe. Masego knew of Louis's reputation from the bosses who traveled to Paris to deal with the jewelers. If he could escape, he would go to Paris to find Louis and work for him, but he needed money and a plan.

"Money was impossible to come by. Obviously, slaves weren't paid. They only got room and board, and those were meager at best. Little by little, he was able to hide gems in a tube in his body . . . a place where the sun doesn't shine, if you get my drift."

Able nodded.

"Masego hid only small gems in the tube except for a relatively large gem. When he had enough gems, he decided to make a run for it. Several others in my family decided to go with him. What could they lose? Either die in the mines, or die trying to escape. One night, three of them left, but the mine bosses hunted them down. Masego's cousins were caught and brought back. They were flogged and speared in front of the workers to set an example. Masego, however, literally ran for days through the woods and mountains, living off the land and meager food he took with him. Many times he thought he would die, but he pressed on.

"In a seaside village, he used the gems to barter his way out of the country and onto a boat. This was very risky because the owners had spread the word that he was on the run. They were just about to catch him when he boarded the boat. He stood on the stern and watched the henchmen on the beach flailing their arms and cursing him as the boat pulled from the dock. He eventually made it to Paris. When he showed Louis his last and largest gem, one he had faceted himself, Louis took Masego on as an apprentice. The stone was a blue African sapphire."

Abel's mind was spinning. "Wow, do you know if it became the center stone in the redesign of Mary of Burgundy's ring?"

Masego jumped up from the table. "What do you know of this ring?"

"I've seen it."

"Seen it? But that's impossible!"

Abel looked around. Patrons were staring at Masego. Abel motioned for him to sit back down. The French jeweler plopped into his chair as though Abel's revelation had taken the life out of him.

"I meant I've seen it on paper," Abel said, not yet willing to reveal the whole story. "My great-grandfather put a sketch of it in a box that was passed down to me. It was in my desk drawer until I recently looked at it."

"But how did your great-grandfather get the sketch? The only copies were given to members of my family who became master jewelers."

The men stared at each other with recognition.

"Could it be one of your relatives came to the United States and settled in New York?" Abel said. "Could it be his name was recorded as Moody instead of Bamudy when he passed through Ellis Island, or that he changed it to Moody to Americanize it?"

The men sat back in thought. There was no question their resemblance wasn't just coincidence. Something stronger connected these two men.

"One of my great-great uncles did immigrate to America," Masego said. "He settled in Brooklyn and worked for an Italian jeweler, but we lost track of him. Could that have been your great-great grandfather?"

"What was his name?" Abel asked.

"In France, it was Lawrence."

"My great-great-grandfather's name was Larry."

Again, all the men could do was stare at each other.

Abel leaned in. "Tell me, why was the sketch given to the others?"

"My family lost track of the ring after it was sold to Queen Catherine de' Medici, but they wanted to reunite it with the family. After all, it was Masego's first setting as an apprentice, so it holds immense significance. They hoped if someone found the ring, they eventually would take it to a jeweler. At the time, jewelers were a tiny group of craftsmen, and they would be able to identify the ring by the sketch if it came into their shop. Of course, now jewelers are on every corner. It would be impossible to distribute the sketch to all of them, even on the internet."

"And if someone found the ring? Then what?"

"We would try to convince the owner to sell it back to us."

"And if they refused?"

"There are other ways of obtaining it." Masego's eyes turned cold, like Abel's coffee.

"What if you learned the ring was cursed?"

"Cursed?" Masego laughed. "Just because Mary died with it on and Catherine de' Medici was an egotistical, power-hungry woman? Unless . . ." Masego leaned forward.

"Unless what?" Abel splayed his hands.

Masego narrowed his eyes to a slit. "Unless you know more than you're letting on."

Abel swallowed hard and glanced at his watch. "Oh no, I had no idea it was so late! I have an appointment and must run. Please excuse me." Abel grabbed his cane and extended his hand. "Thank you for the coffee and history lesson. It's exciting to think we're cousins. I'll check online to see if we've followed the family tree accurately. Wouldn't that be something?"

Masego grasped Abel's hand. "Until we meet again . . . cousin," he said in a slow, deliberate tone with a hint of menace. He squeezed Abel's hand a little too firmly.

At the hotel, Abel showered and changed clothes, then went downstairs where he found Pierre, a bespectacled twenty-something, behind the reception desk.

"How may I help you, monsieur?"

"Do you know anyone I could pay to do some internet research for me?"

"I could do it after my shift. I get off in a half hour. What do you need?"

Abel handed Pierre a piece of paper on which he had drawn his family tree, along with the names, dates and birth cities of his relatives — at least as much as he could remember. "I'd like you to go back as far as you can. I'm looking for a connection to the Masego Bamudy family from France." He pointed at the name on the paper. "I'm told they were here in Paris in the 1500s. You should be able to do some of this on Ancestry.com."

"Yes, I'm familiar with that site, monsieur and the equivalent in France. I put my family's history together for a reunion not long ago."

"Wonderful!" Abel felt fortunate that Pierre was well versed in the sites. He handed him a one hundred euro in appreciation. "This should get you started. If it's more than that, please let me know."

"Very good, monsieur." Pierre stuffed the bill into his pants pocket.

After a two hour nap, Abel noticed a white envelop under his door. Inside were Pierre's findings, along with a note that the money had been sufficient. Abel scanned the research results. Sure enough, Pierre had found the documentation to corroborate that Abel and Masego Bamudy were distant cousins. And the name had been changed to Moody, just as he had surmised.

His descent from slaves who worked in Tanzanian gem mines was quite a revelation, not to mention the ring now at the church contained the gem that the first Masego had smuggled out and faceted. Obviously, he understood why the ring was important to Masego, but he felt it wasn't as important as the history of the women who possessed it. It was that very history he had traveled all the way to Paris to explore and the one that was the catalyst for his mission.

Did Father Albert know all this? He must, because the seventh Masego said the priest had asked about his past. But he couldn't know Abel and Masego were related. Then again, if the woman at the jewelry store noticed their resemblance, why hadn't Father Albert? And how did Father Albert get involved with the ring in the first place?

The only thing Abel knew for sure was that his father had mentioned the priest's name when he warned Abel not to open the paper unless he was going to do something about it: "Contact Father Albert at the Eglise Catholique de Saint-Paul in Paris." His name turned out to be on the first piece of paper in the tin box.

Abel told himself he hadn't come all this way with the ring to allow someone like Masego to take it, regardless of blood ties.

Yes, he would see his mission through.

If he didn't, the cost would be more than he could endure.

Chapter 11

Father Albert opened the side door to let Abel into the church "There you are. I got your note and trust you had a pleasant afternoon."

"Yes, quite pleasant, thank you. I strolled down some charming side streets and did a little window shopping."

Abel and Father Albert walked to the library. Before taking his seat, Father Albert selected several logs from the nearby stack and placed them on the fire. He sat down and picked up *Women of the Ring.*

"Ready for more?" the priest asked, taking his seat.

"Of course, but I've been meaning to ask you something. How did you get interested in the ring?"

Father Albert smiled. "I wondered how long it would take before you asked me that. The fact is I was simply thumbing through old books here in the library that documented past parishioners when I came across Francesca's story. It saddened yet fascinated me, so I continued to follow the thread of her life through the documents and realized there was much more to her story.

"I learned of Mary of Burgundy's ring and of the first Masego through my research. Then, by visiting the shops nearby, I realized the owner of the jewelry shop was also named Masego. We talked, and he told me of the redesigned ring and the story of his relatives in the mines of Tanzania. Oddly enough, about that same time, your father came to Paris. He was just sightseeing but visited the church. I noticed his resemblance to the Bamudy family right away and asked him if he knew anything about a blue African sapphire ring. He told me he had a sketch of the ring and that his family had been looking for it. I told him about my research and how some believed it was cursed. I wrote down my name and phone number and asked him to get in touch with me if the ring ever surfaced."

"So that's how your personal information wound up in the tin box. Now it all makes sense. God works in mysterious ways, doesn't he?" Able smiled and shook his head in amazement.

"Yes, and once I stood at Francesca's grave, the story took on a whole new meaning. It touched my heart and became of utmost importance."

"That's understandable," Abel said, "the story became much more personal to me as well when I stumbled upon her grave this afternoon as I was leaving. But I didn't see a grave for the child. What happened to her?"

"I don't want to give away the next chapter, so I'll let you read it for yourself. I have Mass in about fifteen minutes. You're welcome to attend.

"Thank you, Father, but I need to get back into my reading."

"Very well. I'll check back later, as usual."

Abel smiled. "I'm sure I'll still be here."

~~~

Mosie Boulay

Mosie Boulay kneaded dough at the flour-encrusted table in a khaki dress covered by a white apron, giving orders to the workers in the Tout Délicieux Boulangerie. The nineteen-year-old was running the bakery while her parents were away on holiday for two weeks.

Of course, she had grown up in the shop and learned the business from the ground up, but this was the first time her parents had left her in charge. Undaunted, she relished the opportunity to make subtle changes to improve operations and profitability. In fact, she already was seeing results.

As she glanced up from her kneading, she saw a familiar face enter the kitchen.

"Father Lael, it's so good to see you." Mosie dusted the flour from her hands and pushed wisps of raven hair from her heart-shaped face. She walked from behind the kneading table, threw her arms around the priest whom she regarded as her second father and kissed him on the cheek. "What brings you all this way? I hope it was just to see me." Her blue eyes danced.

"Actually, it is with mixed emotions that I come. Is there some place we can talk in private?"

"Of course, Father, let's go into the office." Mosie led him past rolling carts stacked with French, rye, and sourdough loaves of bread fresh from the oven. The aroma alone would cause a man to salivate.

"You look concerned. Is something wrong?" Mosie gestured to a wooden chair for Father Lael, and she sat opposite him.

Father Lael wrapped his hands around Mosie's floured ones and cleared his throat. "I'm so sorry to tell you this, but I just got word that your parents are no longer with us."

"Of course, they're not," Mosie said with a smile. "They're on holiday."

"That's not what I meant, Mosie. I'm so sorry, but Mr. and Mrs. Boulay are dead."

Mosie angled her head and looked at Father Lael as though she hadn't heard him. When the news sunk in, her eyes brimmed with tears.

"I don't understand. It was the first time they'd been away in years. How could this happen?" Mosie pulled a muslin handkerchief from her apron pocket and blotted her tears.

"They were on a ferry on Lake Geneva southeast of Paris when there was an explosion just as it was about to dock. The ferry sank. Most of the passengers were able to swim to shore or were picked up by boats, but a dozen people perished. Your parents were among them. I'm so very, very sorry." Father Lael's eyes welled with tears, and he cried along with Mosie. "There's something else."

"Something else? More bad news?" How could Father Lael bring her such bad news and then add to it?

"I need to give you something." Father Lael withdrew a small cherry wood box from his pocket and held it in his hand.

"What is it?" Mosie asked.

"It's something your mother left you."

"My mother left something for me at the church?"

"No, my dear, not Mrs. Boulay, this was left by the woman who brought you into this world."

Mosie's brow creased as she looked at Father Lael quizzically. "I knew I was adopted, but I never heard my parents speak about who my mother was or what happened."

"Allow me to tell you what I know." Father Lael cleared his throat and began. "The year was 1665. I was twenty-seven and had been at the parish just one month when all this occurred. Mr. Walker, a farmer, was fishing one morning in the reeds down by the river when he heard some red foxes yipping. He also thought he heard a baby cry. He wondered if he was hearing things, so he went to investigate. He ended up finding a squealing newborn. The baby was in a basket by a tree with a blanket tucked around it.

"Mr. Walker dropped his fishing rod and picked up the basket. He tried to shush the child by rocking it, but he knew it was hungry. He looked around for the mother but didn't find anyone, so he put the basket into his wagon and headed for home. When he reached the fork in the road, he thought better of it, wondering how he and his wife would care for the infant at their age, so he turned his horse north toward the church. By the time he got there, a small crowd that heard the bawling child was following alongside his wagon. When they heard Mr. Walker's explanation of how he'd found the child, they likened the amazing discovery to the biblical story of Moses rescued from the bulrushes. When Mr. Walker reached the steps of the church, I was summoned along with Sisters Nadine and Adele. We took the baby inside."

Mosie leaned in.

"I sent Sister Nadine to fetch Mrs. Lemaire, a midwife who had just had a child of her own. In the meantime, Sister Adele and I spread some clean cloths on the kitchen table and took the child from the blanket so we could wash her with cool water. That's when we discovered the infant was a girl and she had a head full of hair as black as jet.

"When Mrs. Lemaire arrived, she knew just what to do with the bawling child. She cradled the infant in her arm and unbuttoned the top of her dress. The baby stopped crying once the milk began to flow. We had no means to care for the child, so Mrs. Lemaire took the baby home with her while we tried to find her mother. No one ever came forward to claim the child, so we started looking for an adoptive family. It took a year, but we finally found the Boulays."

"So I was the baby in the basket?"

Father Lael nodded.

"But why didn't my parents tell me all this? Surely they knew."

"I encouraged them to do so many times when you were a child, but they never wanted to tell you for some reason. They never said why."

"And my name . . . where did Mosie come from?"

"You were lovingly given that name by the villagers who likened you to a female Moses, discovered in the reeds."

Mosie moved behind her chair. "So who was my mother?"

"No one knows. I guess that, along with the name of your father, will remain a secret. One thing is for sure, though, your real mother loved you very much."

"How can that be? She abandoned me." Mosie turned her back to Father Lael.

"That's true, but she put three very precious things in the basket that day. The first was you. Then there was a note I found pinned to the blanket. At first, I didn't even know it was there. Here, I brought it for you to read."

Mosie turned around with a tear-stained face, and Father Lael handed her an envelope.

Mosie pulled the note out: *Please take care of my baby as I am unable to do so. Use the ring to pay for her care.*

"Ring? What ring?" Mosie asked.

"That was the third thing in the basket. It's in this box. I've been waiting for the right time to give it to you. That time seems now." Father Lael handed the wooden box to her.

"But I don't understand. Why didn't you give it to me before?"

"You didn't need it before. Perhaps now you do."

Mosie's eyes widened as she removed the lid of the box. She lifted the ring and studied it. "It's beautiful."

"I don't know how your mother came into possession of it. I guess that part of the story will forever remain a mystery. The church absorbed the costs of your care until the Boulays adopted you, so I kept the ring, believing there would be a more appropriate time for you to have it. The Boulays' bakery did well, and they seemed able to provide for you without needing the ring. Now that they are gone, perhaps you will need some money for the business or something else."

"But it's the only thing I have of my mother's. I couldn't sell it." A new set of tears cascaded down Mosie's cheeks.

"Perhaps not, but it's yours to do with as you want." Father Lael rose and laid a warm hand on Mosie's shoulder. "I know this is a lot to absorb. Just know that both your birth mother and your adopted one loved you dearly, as do I. If there is anything I can do for you, just say the word. Of course, the parish will make arrangements for your parents to be buried in the church cemetery, and we'll hold the service. But please let me know if there is anything I can do, anything at all."

"Of course, Father. Thank you for your kindness and caring." Mosie wiped her eyes.

"You're very special to me." Father Lael kissed Mosie on the forehead and let himself out.

It took three years for Mosie to get over the shock of her parents' deaths. Through visits and conversations with Father Lael, though, she was able to put the pain behind her and focus on the bakery, which thrived under her savvy leadership. In fact, she enlarged the bakery with a patisserie and hired more staff. Word of her tantalizing pies, tarts, and cakes spread far and wide.

Late one summer afternoon as Mosie was closing up shop alone, a lavish carriage accompanied by four horsemen pulled up in front. From behind the counter, she watched a white-gloved footman in a blue-and-white uniform embellished with gold braid descend the carriage. With great flare, he unfolded the steps of the carriage and opened the door. The first to emerge was a dignified older-aged man in a dark purple valet's uniform. He scanned the sidewalk and spoke to someone in the carriage. A second middle-aged man emerged in white tights and a taupe three quarter-length silk brocade coat with epaulets over matching knickers. Both men walked into the bakery. Mosie's heart raced as she recognized the man.

"Your Majesty." Mosie curtsied. It was her first time seeing the king up close. She was excited and nervous at the same time.

King Philippe didn't look at her. He clasped his hands behind his back and strolled through the bakery, sniffing the air and inspecting trays of croissants and baskets of bread loaves. He circled back to the counter.

"The proprietor, please."

"I am she. Mosie Boulay at your service, sir." She curtsied again.

The king looked at her with skepticism and cleared his throat. "The Boulay's bakery has earned quite a reputation, which has found its way to the palace. I'm told you have outstanding breads and pastries."

"Thank you for the compliment, Your Majesty, but I'm sure others are just as accomplished." Mosie brushed a dark wayward curl away from her face and felt a flush of heat spread across her cheeks.

"I'm looking for something different . . . a new and innovative pastry to serve at my annual ball in November."

"Le tarte tatin is always a crowd pleaser." Mosie smiled. "The apples are firm but not too hard, the caramel sweet and the pastry shell crisp."

Lace ruffles at the end of the king's sleeve swayed as he flicked his long, polished fingers in the air. "Too common. I said I want something different."

Mosie's mind raced. "I might have something, but I'm still working on it. It isn't perfected yet."

"What is it?" the king asked in almost childlike fashion.

"An almond sponge cake layered with ganache and coffee butter cream and covered in a layer of chocolate. I call it l'opera."

"Chocolate? That's for drinking, not for baking!" The king rolled his eyes at his valet, who smirked and nodded in agreement.

"Sir, with all due respect, I've found a way to extract the cocoa butter and reintroduce it to form a frosting that hardens. I just finished putting a cake together. Would you like to taste it?"

"By all means." The king tossed his jet-black wavy hair over his shoulder, and his bushy eyebrows rose over his dark eyes in doubt-tinged expectation.

Mosie strode on unsure legs into the kitchen and returned a few minutes later with a plate bearing a generous wedge of cake. Her hand shook as she handed it, along with a fork and linen napkin, to the king. She leaned against the counter to steady herself.

King Philippe twisted the plate in his hands. He inspected the layers of cream, cake, and unfamiliar chocolate frosting without a hint of emotion. He raised it to his nose and sniffed. Finally, he sliced a large piece with the edge of his fork and slid it into his mouth. He closed his eyes.

Mosie could see his cheek roll as if he was letting the flavors of the cake percolate around his mouth and against his palate and tongue. Her breath caught in her throat, and she felt her palms moisten. Beads of sweat formed on her brow when he didn't comment after the first bite. The king took a second large bite.

A third bite ever bigger.

Still nothing.

Mosie's knees began to quiver.

King Philippe handed the plate with nothing more than crumbs back to Mosie and dabbed the corners of his mouth with the napkin. "Someone will be in touch." Without another word, the king and his valet exited the bakery and climbed back into the carriage.

Mosie slid down the counter, still holding the empty plate, until she sprawled on the floor, legs out in front of her. She let out a heavy sigh of relief. The king was gone, but had he liked the cake?

A week later, she received a note from the king. He directed her not to amend the recipe of l'opera and told her he would feature it as the culinary highlight of the fall ball. He would send a carriage for her two weeks prior to the event to take her to the palace, where she would stay until the ball was over. She would order the ingredients and direct the staff in making the recipe. She was not to breathe a word about the cake to anyone in the meantime. After the ball, she could make it available to the public.

For the next two months, Mosie concentrated on purchasing enough cocoa beans to make the frosting and multiplying the ingredients to serve the two hundred and fifty anticipated guests. She also convinced the king to allow her to bring four of her bakers to ensure the cake would be exceptional.

Father Lael called on her three days before she was to leave. With all the excitement and arrangements to be away from the bakery for two weeks, she hadn't had time to visit him but did send a note about her plans.

"We spend much too much time apart," Mosie said before planting a kiss on his cheek.

"Yes, and it seems you become more beautiful every time I see you."

Mosie blushed. She knew her beauty at twenty-five wasn't what it used to be, but she was grateful she would always be young and attractive in Father Lael's eyes.

"How about a stroll in the park?" Father Lael asked. "It's a lovely day, and all too soon it will turn bitter. Today, there's a cool breeze but warm sun. Perfect for walking."

Mosie left instructions with her staff and grabbed her shawl. She and Father Lael chatted about things back in the village until they found a bench and sat down. Mosie tipped her head back and let the sun warm her pale cheeks. She closed her eyes and smiled as the warmth spread down to her toes.

"The sun feels so good. You'd think I've been living in a cave."

"Well, I'm sure your job doesn't leave you much time for getting out and meeting people," Father Lael said.

"No, but the answer to your unspoken question is yes, I have met a couple of widowers. But nothing serious."

Father Lael turned to Mosie and took her hands.

"Every time you do that, you deliver bad news," Mosie said.

"My child, since God is in control, and we don't know his thoughts or the plans he has for us, news is neither good nor bad, it simply is. I liken it to the weather. One person is thankful for the rain while another curses it."

"So what is it you want to tell me?"

Father Lael gazed out to the stand of aspens that lined the park. The last of their golden leaves sparkled in the sun and clung desperately to the branches while the breeze tried to loosen them.

"A woman died in the village two days ago. Her name was Carmen. She gave me a letter as I administered last rights and said I was to read it after she was gone. When I did, the circumstances surrounding your mother, the ring, and your being found as an infant in the basket all came together. She gave me this letter to give to you." Father Lael withdrew a creased cream colored envelope from inside his jacket pocket and handed it to Mosie.

She opened it with trepidation and read the three pages in silence. Then she folded the letter and tucked it back into the envelope.

"So my mother's name was Francesca Grimaldi, and after giving birth to me, she walked into the river and drowned herself?"

Father Lael nodded.

"Why didn't she take me with her?"

"Her shame was more than she could bear, and leaving you with her mother would have also brought shame to her. You were an innocent child. How could she transfer her shame to you?"

"Who else knows about this?"

"No one. As you can see, I've been charged with making sure no one ever finds out."

"I can't believe the king is my father! He raped my mother, and she killed herself out of shame." Mosie's face and eyes grew hard.

"Just remember, Mosie, while you see it as a tragedy, something very good came out of it: you. That's not tragic at all; it's a blessing."

"Are you trying to tell me this wasn't a tragedy all the way around?"

"I'm trying to say God can use tragic situations to bless others. That's what happened in your case. Out of what you consider a tragedy, you were born, lived, and blessed the lives of the Boulays, your employees, your friends, and me. Don't let bitterness rob you of joy."

Mosie sighed. "Thank you, Father, for your words. I'll certainly consider them." She kissed Father Lael on the cheek and walked back with him to the bakery in silence.

Three days later, Mosie and her staff boarded a carriage that would take them to the palace. Once there, she proceeded to instruct the bakery staff, order the ingredients, and meticulously plan out the process so the staff would know exactly how to perform their duties. She and a staff of seven also rehearsed twice to perfect the serving time.

When the big day came, Mosie helped the ten kitchen staff cut and plate the cakes. She had made a smaller cake exclusively for the king with an extra special ingredient and elaborate chocolate garnishes. From this, she cut the king a generous slice.

"Make sure the king gets this slice. It came from the cake I made especially for him," she said, as she handed the tray with the plated cake to the male server.

"Of course," he replied.

When the servers returned to the kitchen, they told her how the guests had raved about the featured dessert. She was greatly pleased.

After the ball, word of the featured cake found a willing audience, and it was difficult for Mosie's shop to keep up with the demand. Early one morning while Mosie was bent down putting l'opera cakes into the pastry case, Mr. Dubin, the next-door merchant, burst through the door all out of breath.

"Mosie, have you heard? King Philippe is dead! They say he was poisoned. Arsenic."

Mosie hid a sly grin before she straightened with a feigned gasp. "Why Mr. Dubin, how horrible!"

"Yes, I must tell the others!" Mr. Dubin left as quickly as he arrived.

The next day, Father Lael arrived at the bakery and invited Mosie out for a walk in the park despite the overcast sky and chilly wind. They sat on the same bench as before, gazing at the aspens. Their branches were devoid of leaves this time. Winter had won.

"They'll find out, Mosie," Father Lael said in a calm voice. "It's only a matter of time."

"He deserved to die for what he did to my mother." Mosie stared out at the trees, her face as expressionless as the stark limbs.

"Perhaps, but this wasn't the way, and God did not appoint you to be the executioner."

"She was only fourteen, Father. Fourteen! She didn't deserve any of it."

"That's true, Mosie, but God takes care of these things in his own way. He doesn't want or need your help."

"His way was to let the king go on about his business."

Father Lael sighed. "I know it appears that way, but God knows things far beyond our comprehension."

"Well, anyway, it's done. All you can do now, Father, is pray for my soul."

"I will do that, my child."

Several days later, Mosie wrote Father Lael:

January 17, 1696

Dear Father Lael,

The palace guards have questioned me, and I think they will arrest me any day now. Please know that you have been a wonderful friend, the most valuable and stable person in my life. I don't regret leaving this earth, if that is my fate, only leaving you.

Occasionally, I take out my mother's ring and look at it, but I've never worn it, as it would invoke far too many questions . . . ones I couldn't bear to answer. I can't help but think none of this would have happened if she hadn't removed it from the palace ceiling — a cursed tribulation she sadly endured.

I baked the ring into a loaf of bread that went out for delivery. I don't know where it went, but I hope the next person who gets it will have better fortune than did my mother or I.

Your loving "daughter,"
Mosie

~~~

The story ended there, but Abel noticed several notes Father Albert had clipped to the page, all copies of the originals. The first was the note Francesca had pinned to the baby's blanket. The second was Carmen's letter to Mosie. The third was written by Father Lael. Father Albert had translated all three into English. Abel read each with considerable interest, especially the last one.

That the richness of the life God intended for Mosie was lost by her bitterness and bad choices saddens me to the depths of my soul. That her mother, Francesca, deliberately lost her life in the river was bad enough, but that Mosie was publicly beheaded for her crime against the king was almost more than I could endure. I know somehow God will use it all for His glory, but I can't possibly understand how that will happen at this moment.

Father Lael

Abel closed the book. The last chapter had drained him. In many ways, his feelings echoed Father Lael's — that Mosie's let bitterness cut her life short was a tragedy. On the other hand, he understood her desire for retribution after what the king had done to her mother. Raised by God-fearing parents, however, he relied on his belief that God took care of these things in his own way and all we could do was live as righteous a life as possible.

Thirsty, Abel walked to the kitchen, where he found Father Albert nibbling on a sliced apple at the table. "How was Mass?" Abel asked.

"It was a smaller crowd than usual, but my message seemed to touch several parishioners. At least, that's what they said."

Abel selected a bottle of water from the shelf and sat opposite Father Albert. "Father, do you believe in curses?"

"What you really mean is do I believe the ring is cursed?"

"Well, yes. It seems terrible things happened to all the women who possessed it or their families."

"I think the bigger question is whether an object can carry a curse that taints the person who possesses it, or whether the things that happen to people are due to their choices or simply a byproduct of life?"

"Ah, yes, I guess that's really the bigger question. Well, what do you think? Can an object carry a curse?"

"Let's keep that discussion for another time. I have some pressing parish matters tonight, and you need to finish the book. In the end, you may be able to answer the question yourself. If nothing else, you'll have a bit more insight."

"Perhaps you're right, but I'm tired and want to head back to the hotel. I'll return in the morning, though, if that is convenient for you?"

"Quite convenient. Shall I have breakfast for you?"

"That is so kind of you, Father Albert. I'll be here at 8:00 a.m. sharp."

Chapter 12

A square contemporary glass clock over the reception desk chimed 10:00 p.m. as Julia and Winston entered Hotel Caron in Paris and scanned the quiet lobby painted in a soft gray.

The reception desk, embellished with black iridescent tile, stood directly across from the entrance. An arched entry to the left led to a breakfast nook resembling a stone grotto. A Chinese couple talked quietly in dark-gray leather side chairs in a corner, and a uniformed employee walked through on the way to his duties. No one else was around besides the front desk clerk, Danielle.

Julia stood by Winston as he filled out a registration form for Danielle, and she handed them two card keys for room 405.

"The lift is just across the lobby." Danielle pointed at the elevator opposite the front desk and next to the entry.

"We're friends with Mr. Abel Moody and want to surprise him. Do you know if he is in?" Julia asked.

"I'm sorry, madam, we don't keep track of our guests, but I'll be happy to call his room."

"No, that's okay. Could you tell us what room he's in so we can call him later?"

"I'm sorry, we don't give out that information."

"Well, please don't tell him we asked about him. We don't want to spoil the surprise." She winked at Danielle as they headed for the elevator.

Their compact room matched the lobby's same soft gray. Floor-to-ceiling gold damask curtains accented a window overlooking the street. A small black desk and chair were nestled in a corner next to the bed, and a black dresser hugged the wall at the foot of the bed. A flat-screen TV hung above it.

"So, how are we going to find Mr. Moody, and if we do, what do we do then?" Winston sat on the bed and pulled off his shoes.

"I don't have all that figured out, but we do need to find out what's going on."

"We could be here for days and never see him."

"I guess that's possible. If we have no luck for a couple of days, we'll just enjoy Paris and our time together." Julia kissed Winston on the cheek before walking to the window to look out to the road below. A street lamp about a block away illuminated a dark-skinned figure with a cane walking toward the hotel. "It's him!" She pointed out the window.

Winston rushed to her side. "Are you sure?"

"Positive. Hurry down to the lobby! See where he goes."

Winston slipped his shoes back on and bolted out the door. Julia watched Mr. Moody cross the street and enter the hotel. She hoped Winston had made it to the lobby in time to see where he went. A few minutes later, he entered the room.

"What happened?" Julia asked.

"Well, I pretended to be looking at brochures from the display. When he got on the elevator, I followed him. We had a brief conversation."

"So? What did you learn?"

Winston shrugged. "Not much. Mr. Moody isn't sightseeing, but he indicated it's not business either. What's between a vacation and business?"

"Something very personal." Julia furrowed her brow. "And we need to find out just what that is. Let's get a good night's sleep, and we'll follow him in the morning."

Julia and Winston arose at 6:30 a.m. so they wouldn't miss Mr. Moody. The breakfast nook they had seen the night before sat about fourteen people at small glass-topped tables with chrome chairs upholstered in white vinyl. On a narrow continental breakfast bar were a pitcher of orange and grapefruit juice, a dozen mini boxes of granola, a bowl of ice with cartons of milk, two baskets of croissants and donuts, and a bowl of mixed fruit. A French baguette sat on a shelf above a toaster. An attendant was on hand to replenish the food and assist guests.

As they ate, Winston kept an eye out for Mr. Moody in case he left the hotel. When they finished, he took up vigil in a lobby chair and perused the pamphlets he had picked up the night before. Julie lingered at the table with a pamphlet on the Eiffel Tower. She would use it to cover her face should Mr. Moody come in for breakfast.

As she waited for Winston's cue that Mr. Moody was on the move, Julie reflected on the situation. She had never known Mr. Moody to be devious or untrustworthy, yet she was about to tail him like some detective after a criminal! It all felt odd and bizarre. She wasn't proud of what she was doing, but what else could she do? After all, he had left Brooklyn under suspicious circumstances on a one-way flight immediately after looking at her ring. What could be more fishy than that?

"He's heading out," Winston said as he rushed to the table.

Julia grabbed her bag, and they followed ten yards behind Mr. Moody, trying to blend in with pedestrians on the sidewalk. After three blocks, they watched him walk through a cemetery and enter an old stone church.

"Wonder what he's doing in there?" Julia asked.

"No clue, now what?" Winston said.

"Let's hang around to see if he comes out. If he doesn't, let's stroll down the side streets and see what Paris is all about."

Julia and Winston toured the headstones, vaults, and elaborate statuary in the cemetery making sure they kept one eye on the door in case Mr. Moody came out. After an hour with no sign of him, they left. As they were walking back to the hotel, they came upon a jewelry store. The name on the sign said Babioles et Jijoux. Underneath it in smaller print was the English translation: Baubles & Jewels.

"Let's take a look," Winston said. "After all, we may end up needing another engagement ring. Perhaps they'll have something unique."

Julia froze with her mouth agape as they approached the door.

"Winston, look at their logo!" She pointed at an image of a ring on a decal that was being adhered to the front window.

"It's our ring!" Winston said.

The couple looked at each other wide-eyed. Julia pulled the printout of the ring from her bag.

"Why, it's the spitting image, right down to the symbols painted in gold between the smaller gems! Just what's going on here?" Julia felt heat prickle up her neck.

"Let's act like we're looking for a ring and play it cool. I'll do the talking."

In a huff, Julia stuffed the printout back in her purse.

"Bonjour," said the female clerk behind the counter.

"Bonjour, do you speak English?" Winston asked.

"Yes, how may I help you?"

"We're looking for an engagement ring. We want something different and saw your logo being placed on the front door. Is that ring available? It's perfect for what we had in mind." Winston turned to Julia who issued a broad smile and nodded her agreement.

"*Désolé.* So sorry, but that is a ring from many centuries ago. We don't have that ring in the store, but perhaps our master jeweler can make you a similar one. Allow me to get him."

Before they could respond, the clerk exited through a door behind the counter. A few seconds later, a man with skin as dark as Abel's and wearing a jeweler's apron approached them from the same door.

Julia's forehead crinkled as she looked at the jeweler. Something was very familiar about him. Where did she know him from?

"Bonjour, I am Masego Bamudy, the master jeweler and owner. I understand you're looking for an engagement ring and were inquiring about the one in our logo?"

"Yes, it's quite unusual, and that's what we're looking for," Winston said. "We understand you don't have it, but we're curious about its history. Your clerk said it's from centuries ago. My fiancé and I both liked it immediately. We're into antiques."

"It's a family heirloom crafted by one of my great uncles back in the sixteenth century, but unfortunately, we lost track of it over the centuries."

"The little gold symbol between the jewels fascinates me. Do you know what it is?" Julia looked at Masego expectantly.

"It's a falcon with its wings outstretched — to honor the owner of the original ring, Mary of Burgundy. She was a falconer."

"A falconer, how interesting!" Julia clapped her hands and raised her brows at Winston.

"Yes, we'd love to find the ring," Masego said.

"I'm sure that is nearly impossible after so many years. It could be anywhere," Winston said.

"True, but I have a lead."

"Really? Tell us about it." Julia leaned in, but Masego drew back and changed the subject.

"Now, may I show you something else?"

Winston looked at Julia, who stuck out her lower lip in a big pout.

"Uh, my fiancée and I have our hearts set on something similar to the ring in your logo. Your clerk said you might be able to make a replica," Winston said.

"I'm sorry, but that's impossible. There is only one ring like that."

"But you do make jewelry here, don't you?" Winston said.

"Of course, monsieur. Anything except for a replica of that particular ring." Masego's dark eyes punctuated his resolution with a heavy stare.

"Well, thank you for your time. We'll keep looking."

After they walked out, Julia stopped to take a photo of the logo with her camera. Masego glared at her through the window.

"What's our next move?" Winston asked.

"I'm not sure. What I do know, though, is something very odd is going on here. Is it mere coincidence that we've arrived in Paris only to find a replica of our engagement ring being stuck on a store window? And is it coincidence that we met the jeweler whose family actually fashioned the ring centuries ago and says he has a lead on where it is? This situation is becoming more bizarre by the moment. Let's head back to the church and see if we can find Mr. Moody. We really need to talk to him."

Chapter 13

From the kitchen table, Abel inhaled the aroma of tangy orange sauce with Grand Marnier warming in a pan on the stove. Father Albert was whisking batter at the counter for thin French crepes. Fresh strawberries and orange juice were already on the table in front of Abel.

"I can't wait to dig into your gourmet breakfast or find out who got the loaf of bread and the ring." Abel popped a strawberry into his mouth from the bowl. Perfect — a ripe red berry sweet with flavor. He knew France didn't grow strawberries in the winter but was thankful Florida, Spain, and South America could grow such wonderful produce while the rest of the U.S. and Europe were dominated by cold weather or perhaps even snow.

"You may be disappointed," Father Albert said. He poured his batter into two large round shallow pans and swirled them to spread the batter.

"What do you mean?"

Father Albert waited to answer until he lightly browned the crepes on both sides. He rolled them up and dribbled spoonfuls of orange sauce on top. He set one in front of Abel and the other at his place. He finally answered the question after offering grace.

"Though I searched and searched, I never discovered who found the ring in the loaf of bread. Two decades passed before the ring showed up in the late 1700s in the hands of a fascinating woman who played a clandestine role in the French Revolution. That was a horrible time, but the revolt proved a necessary evil and a vital part of our country's and the world's history. It led to the elimination of the feudal system and initiated government by elected representatives. It set the political tone for Europe and the rest of the world."

"I'm afraid I don't remember my world history enough to realize its impact, but I did see *Les Miserables*, the Broadway musical about the revolution. So our next ring bearer was somehow involved in the rebellion?" Abel drained his glass of orange juice.

"Yes, quite a remarkable woman. But I'll let you read all about her." Father Albert wiped his mouth with a napkin and nodded at Abel's empty plate. "Would you like another crepe?"

"No, thanks. It was wonderful, of course, but quite enough. Don't need this waistline to expand any more." He patted his middle, and let out a warm chuckle. "I'll just be off to the library to finish my reading. Can I help you clean up first?"

"No, don't worry about it. I'll check back with you later."

"Would appreciate that, Father."

Abel hoped he wouldn't fall asleep in front of the toasty fire after such a delicious meal. Once he read the first page of the next chapter, though, he realized he wouldn't have to worry about that. Father Albert apparently was right about her.

~~~

Grace Dalrymple Elliott

Grace watched Father Durand make the sign of the cross, smile, and speak the final words of the wedding ceremony: "By the powers vested in me by France and the pope, I declare you husband and wife." She felt her new husband's lips upon hers and silently prayed they would forge a successful marriage. With the hard, almost conquering impression left on her soft pursed lips, though, she wasn't so sure.

Grace Dalrymple Elliott's slender frame, straight posture, attractive heart-shaped face, brown eyes and powdered auburn hair had immediately attracted Dr. John Elliott in 1774. He, considerably shorter than her five-foot, seven-inch frame, was heavy set with a robust, unpleasant face dominated by a large nose and dark, bushy eyebrows.

Grace had feigned attraction for the man nearly twenty years her senior because she knew as an eighteen-year-old she had little to say about her future. Although she appreciated her father's efforts in arranging the marriage with her financial stability in mind, she knew income from her husband's flourishing medical practice and his prestige as a physician weren't enough to make a happy marriage. She'd seen dozens of well-off marriages fail while others with little money flourished because of the partners' unfailing commitment to each other.

In the receiving line at the reception, Grace smiled and graciously accepted congratulations and blessings upon her marriage from Father Durand, her father, sister, brother, and guests. Still, how long would it last when their backgrounds were so different?

She had lived a sheltered life, one privileged yet absent of a close family bond. It was because of this upbringing, she surmised, that the marriage had been thrust upon her so she could have some semblance of stability. Her parents had separated before she was born in Scotland. When she was eleven, her mother died of tuberculosis, so Grace was sent to live with her father in London. He, in turn, arranged for her to live at a convent boarding school in Paris. After dropping her off and just before his return to London, her father presented her with a blue sapphire ring. He called it, "a token of his love and affection."

Grace both cherished and loathed the ring. She loved it for its beauty and connection to her father, but she also hated it for being a surrogate gift, a replacement for her father's presence and devotion.

She studied hard and proved to be a good student with a curious mind and the ability to think independently. She excelled in her etiquette classes and made friends easily. Yet she missed her father despite her academic and social successes.

After five years at the convent where she received an outstanding education and practiced her social graces, she returned to London and lived with her father for three years until she married Dr. Elliott.

Grace knew her husband had grown up in a middle-class family who expressed high hopes for him. He had studied hard for four years and eventually met his family's expectations, emerging with medical training and a burgeoning practice. His reputation as an excellent physician grew along with his client list that now encompassed royalty, including the Prince of Wales, son of King George III. His standing in the community had led to invitations to membership in the prestigious King's Club, prominent events, and royal parties. Grace usually accompanied him, although she would go unescorted if he was called away to see a patient.

On one of those occasions two months after her wedding, Grace stood alone by the grand piano in Lord Ashton of Hyde's ballroom watching the dancing. The party, to celebrate his wife's fiftieth birthday, was a gay affair for everyone, including Arthur Raskins, a respected barrister who advocated for his clients in the highest court.

Grace, wearing a cream-colored off-the-shoulder silk dress with black embroidery around the hemline, watched from across the room as the barrister threw back his head and laughed heartily at something the couple beside him said. When his eyes caught Grace's, he gulped down the remnants of his Champagne, excused himself, and staggered over to her. He leaned heavily against the piano while his hazy eyes swept over her like a potential lover.

"And just where is that rascal John tonight? I see he's left his beautiful new bride again to fend for herself." His hand brushed across a silver tray carried by a passing uniformed and white-gloved server to deposit his Champagne glass and snatch another filled with the bubbly.

"Duty calls. You know his patients always come first," Grace said in singsong voice, forcing a smile. It was all she could do to keep her composure. Her heart always sank when her husband was summoned away just as they were getting ready for bed or dressing for a party.

Raskins scanned the room. He leaned in and spoke in a whisper laced with the noxious odor of alcohol. "Yes, well, I'm sure you know his bedside manner is more than that of doctor-patient relationship." He punctuated his accusation with a wink.

Grace's eyes grew wide as she touched her neckline and gasped. "Whatever do you mean, Mr. Raskins?"

"Oh, it's common knowledge, my dear. Your husband gives great physicals . . . to both women and men." His eyes proved glassy as he raised the Champagne glass to his lips and drained it in one gulp.

Grace stiffened. She had speculated her husband's excessively long house calls day or night might be more than professional, but no one had spoken so candidly before.

"Excuse me, Mr. Raskins, but I need some refreshment." Grace's lips clamped into a thin red line. As she headed toward the buffet table, she stumbled when Raskins's long fingers wrapped around her arm in restraint. Her eyes narrowed at him in disdain.

His eyelids drooped like a partially pulled shade, and an upturn at the corner of his mouth formed a sly grin. "Just remember, my dear, two can play this game," he said in a deliberate tone tainted with a slur. "With your youth, beauty, and sophistication, I'm sure many a man would cherish your company, unlike your husband." He took her hand and pressed his pursed lips on the back of it leaving a wet tattoo.

Heat surged through Grace as she yanked her hand away and threaded her way through the crowd. While she was disgusted by his suggestion, oddly, it piqued something inside of her at the same time. Why shouldn't she enjoy another's company just like her husband?

Five months later, the wife of a prominent businessman invited her to lunch at In The Garden. Grace knew of the restaurant, of course, but not being of Britain's upper crust, she had never been there.

Ten tables were strategically placed throughout the elaborate dining room, close enough to be intimate, yet far enough away for discrete conversation. Fine linen taupe tablecloths overlaid with white ones complemented

Waterford crystal glasses and Wedgwood china. A formal English garden was painted in the oval tray ceiling. It depicted fountains and arbors sprinkled throughout sculpted symmetric hedges accented by pink tulips, purple lavender, and yellow roses. The inset was edged in gold leaf, and four crystal chandeliers hung at the border of the tray ceiling.

The maître d' escorted Grace to a corner table where Mrs. Geraldine Haig was waiting. Her fast-paced chatter about the weather, fashion, and dinner party invitations exposed her nervousness to Mrs. Haig, whose husband owned the Haig and McTavish Distillery. Though she always found Mrs. Haig very proper and kind, they didn't have much in common. Why would a woman more than twice her age invite her to lunch?

Mrs. Haig was high society, almost royalty, and had grandchildren. Grace was upper middle class, barely twenty with no children. Their only connection was that they were wives of prominent men who belonged to the same club, and they socialized at parties. After a lull, Mrs. Haig turned the conversation to a more personal nature, finally offering a clue behind her motivation.

"Grace, dear, I hope what I'm about to say will be taken as motherly advice in a gesture of friendship, not judgment. I've noticed your demeanor at some of the parties has turned quite . . . how shall I say it? . . . quite familiar toward the men. While it's acceptable for husbands to have affairs outside the confines of marriage, the opposite situation would be considered matrimonial heresy and most damaging to one's reputation, not to mention financial suicide." Mrs. Haig's hazel eyes peered at Grace over the edge of her rose-embellished porcelain teacup as she sipped chamomile tea.

Grace's breath caught in her throat by Mrs. Haig's boldness. She took a sip of water. "What are you trying to say, Mrs. Haig?"

"I'm trying to say, Grace dear, that it would be in your best interest to be more careful, more reserved. Believe me, you don't want people noticing that you're being so friendly with the men."

Grace swallowed hard and replied in a low, trembling voice with a distinct edge of defiance. "It's acceptable for men to seek outside companionship from a tepid wife, but for a woman to do that, well, that is simply shameful?"

Mrs. Haig leaned in with a smile. "Yes," she said unapologetically. "Right or not, it's just the way things are." She dabbed at the corners of her mouth with a white linen napkin.

Grace took a deep breath and exhaled slowly. She leaned in and spoke just above a whisper in a friendly yet firm tone. "The double standard is hard to swallow. Why, do you know John already has sired one illegitimate child during the two years of our marriage? And rumors of his dalliances are flying around like game birds on the run. Certainly, that doesn't make for matrimonial bliss. I now sleep in a separate bedroom, as the thought of him touching me turns my stomach!"

Grace's anger and resentment finally had bubbled over, and she was astonished she had just divulged such intimate secrets to a mere acquaintance! But then, gossip travelled fast in their small circle. She probably wasn't telling Mrs. Haig anything she didn't already know.

"That may be, dear, but flaunting yourself at every eligible bachelor and married man is setting yourself up for gossip and stories of the most sorted kind. It could lead to something far worse. Believe me, it's not what a woman of your status wants." Mrs. Haig refreshed her tea with cream and a teaspoon of brown sugar.

Grace sat back against the needlepoint upholstered Louis XIV chair and relaxed her tense shoulders. Was she moving too fast? The tug of attention and affection from a man, the intoxication she had yearned for at home, was difficult, if not impossible, to ignore. Still young and attractive, she needed to feel wanted, appreciated. She craved a man's touch, his embrace, his kiss, and what followed. She didn't want to miss out on any of what she believed were life's greatest pleasures.

"Thank you for your advice, Mrs. Haig," Grace said in a tone as appreciative as possible. "I realize you're only trying to help, but my needs are greater than what my unfaithful husband can provide."

Mrs. Haig gently squeezed Grace's hand from across the table. "Well, my dear, consider yourself forewarned."

"Oh, father, why did you leave me when I was so young? I needed you then, and I need you now. Your absence has been most painful and your death most cruel." Grace sat on the edge of her bed holding the sapphire ring in her open palm.

With her and John living separate lives, little communication with her siblings, and her father's tragic death from a heart attack a month ago, she felt entirely alone. Oh, how she wished she were seventeen again and living back at her father's house, where she felt protected and loved, even though her father had demonstrated his affection primarily with gifts.

She watched as the fading sun cast prisms of light around the room from the gems and slipped the ring onto her finger. As unrealistic as it might be, she felt her father's presence and support. She hoped tonight's party, which she would attend alone once again, would lead her to a man with whom she could find true happiness. But feeling emotionally and physically abandoned, she knew she was vulnerable to any attention that might come her way.

The party turned out uneventful. Disappointed, she stopped in at a London bagnio for coffee before returning home. A man approached her table while she was deep in thought.

"Are you alone?"

Grace looked up into the handsome face of a well-dressed gentleman who appeared close to her age.

"Allow me to introduce myself. I'm Lord Valentia." He nodded politely. "And you are?"

"Mrs. John Elliot." She extended her hand, and he tenderly kissed the back of it.

"Would you mind some company? I hate to see a woman, even a married one, sitting alone in a coffee shop." His blue eyes appeared friendly and engaging.

"Not at all. I could use some company." Grace gestured for him to sit opposite her.

Their conversation was lighthearted and filled with laughter that whisked her away into another world free from her problems. As the night wore on, she found herself relishing his company — so much so that she promised to meet him again when they parted. Before long, the two ignited a passionate relationship through clandestine rendezvous where they immersed themselves in each other.

Of course, Grace tried to keep the affair secret, but she discovered a year and a half into it that John suspected infidelity and had hired a private investigator. It was only a matter of time before she was exposed.

"You wanted to see me?" Grace detested being in the presence of her husband and avoided him unless they had something of great importance to discuss. She waited in an upholstered side chair while John paced the sitting room, hands clasped behind his back.

Finally, he gripped each arm of her chair and leaned in until his rotund face was but inches from hers. Grace studied the spider veins in his flushed cheeks, the fire in his eyes, and the quiver of his lips.

"Your affair with Lord Valentia has become an embarrassment to me, the family, and the Elliott name. I won't stand for it!"

Grace could feel John's hot breath on her cheeks, and she jerked back at his every word to avoid his spittle.

"I'm sending you out of the city to the country house for nine months. I want to ensure no child is the byproduct of your adulterous and scandalous affair. In the meantime, I will be filing for divorce and suing your lover for Criminal Conversation."

"You wouldn't dare!" As Grace yelled, Mrs. Haig's warning rang in her ears.

"It's already done!" John roared back. "Pack your bags, the carriage is waiting!" He turned on his heels and stormed off.

Grace felt shaken. Their tumultuous marriage finally had erupted. Although she would have preferred the ending to have been on her terms, she was relieved and grateful she would no longer be under his dominion.

She waited two years for John's petition of divorce to move through the courts. First, it was presented to the ecclesiastical court for the legal separation, then it went to civil court for declaration of damages. In 1776, it was presented to the House of Lords in Parliament for final approval. King George III subsequently signed off on the dissolution.

John was awarded twelve thousand pounds in damages from the estate of Lord Valentia and the right to remarry. Grace was granted an allowance of two hundred pounds per year, a mere pittance on which to support the lavish life style to which she was accustomed.

Abandoned by her friends and family and with her reputation in tatters, Grace was now considered a member of the demimonde, the name given to women living on the fringes of acceptable society. With the loss of her social status and no means of support other than her trifling allowance, she was forced to survive as a courtesan — the much earlier suggestion by Mr. Raskins coming to fruition.

Instead of withering on the vine of unacceptability, however, she climbed higher up the ladder of British society with each affair. She reached one of the highest rungs when she met Lord George James Cholmondeley, 1st Marquess of Cholmondeley, at a masquerade ball in the rotunda at the Pantheon, a popular entertainment venue on the south side of Oxford Street in London. She knew of him, of course, but they had never met until the handsome eligible bachelor of considerable wealth and prestige strode across the room and bowed his tall frame courteously to her.

"May I have this dance?" He was dressed in black pants, silk brocade waistcoat, and black velvet jacket embellished with gold cord. His eyes sparkled behind his black sequined-and-feather mask as he caught Grace's gaze.

"Of course." She curtsied in her dark pink dress overlaid with a lighter pink skirt in silk brocade adorned at the edges with lace. The long beaded sleeves were cuffed in lace, and three light pink bows descended in size down the front of the bodice.

Their initial allemande to a ten-piece string ensemble led to a series of dances with music composed by Couperin, Purcell, Bach, and Handel. By the time the evening ended, Lord Cholmondeley was enamored with Grace, and she with him.

"May I see you home?" Lord Cholmondeley asked.

"Of course," Grace said, trying to contain her excitement.

The two became thoroughly absorbed in each other as the night wore into morning. The relationship blossomed, and they appeared well-suited for each other. Lord Cholmondeley was so taken with Grace that he commissioned Thomas Gainsborough, one of the leading artists of the day, to paint her full portrait. In the pose, her blue sapphire ring from her father graced her right middle finger.

Months of courtship turned into four years. While marriage seemed the next logical step, no proposal materialized. Grace was heartbroken that the prospect of her future as Lady Cholmondeley was over, and she needed a change of scenery. In 1779, she moved to France, where she continued to market herself as a high-class courtesan.

After ten months of separation, Lord Cholmondeley traveled to France to reestablish his relationship with Grace. He convinced her to return with him back to England, but their renewed liaison was short lived. Despite being at odds regarding matrimony, the two remained friendly, with Lord Cholmondeley evolving into her protector.

Grace sat across from George in his sitting room in richly upholstered chairs. She had been invited to tea at his home, as they had not seen each other in more than seven months.

"Is it true?" George asked.

Grace lifted her chin, raised her teacup, and sipped the hot refreshment. "Yes, it's true. My daughter was born March 30."

"And rumor of the father?"

"That's true too – the Prince of Wales.

"I hear he has not accepted the child as his."

"He hasn't denied her either. His generous annual annuity attests to that."

Silence stretched between the former lovers.

George cleared his throat. "I understand her skin is of a dark caramel color. Is it possible she's someone else's child . . . even mine?"

Having been with a number of men, Grace knew the timing of the child's birth put him and other members of the British royalty well within the realm of possibility.

Grace raised an eyebrow and shrugged. "Regardless, it's been settled. My daughter has been christened Georgiana Augusta Frederica Seymour, after the prince, and he's listed as the father on her christening record."

"How will you take care of her? It's not as though you can bring her up yourself."

"I'm not at all sure." Grace's voice drifted off as did her eyes, and her brow drew into a knot. It was the first time she had pondered how she would juggle the demands of an infant and those of her well-paying clients.

George leaned forward. "My dear, please let me help you. Let me raise her for you."

Grace tossed him a skeptical look. "Whatever possessed you to make such an offer?"

"You know you're very special to me. I'd do anything for you."

"Anything except marry me." Grace shot him an icy stare.

"We've been through all that, Grace. Regardless of my feelings for you, my future and legacy is determined by tradition."

"Of course, and you must make sure to carefully protect that tradition." Grace turned her head away.

"Back to the child, Grace. Think of her. Think of her future."

Grace walked to the window and pulled back the heavy red velvet curtain to look out onto the lush garden. An upward curve replaced the straight line of her lips as she envisioned her daughter laughing while playing on the plush green grass.

"You're right, of course. It's Georgiana's life I must think of." She hesitated before letting the curtain fall back and turning to George. "All right, I accept your offer. But you must bring her to see me in France occasionally."

George nodded his agreement.

Grace returned to France and resumed her life as a courtesan. She wrote George regularly and saw her daughter twice a year. In 1791, Grace sent him a letter explaining the desperate situation in Paris:

Dearest George,

I'm sure you've heard that what was once law and order in France has deteriorated into frightening chaos, and the revolution that for years seethed under the surface is now upon us. Subtle at first, the anarchy has now become a reign of terror in the streets.

French citizens were being crushed by high taxes and put upon by the nobility. They wanted a more representative government and demanded an end to the feudal system. It has turned into a mighty clash between royalists and commoners — the haves and have-nots. The commoners have taken it into their own hands to nullify what stood for centuries. While I cannot blame them for their anger, still, the resulting uprising is frightening beyond words. Anyone associated with the French court seems to be fair game, despite their lack of influence or their only crime being born into royalty or a relative of a royal. Even the Duke de Orleans (Egalite), with whom I have been in an intimate relationship for years, has turned on the government and his cousin the King.

Swiss Guards and the battalion of St. Thomas who guarded the King were cut to pieces, many beheaded by the overwhelming and angry citizenry. The king's innocent servants were murdered by the lawless mob and the Palace pillaged. The king wasn't there at the time, but as soon as they locate him, I'm sure his life will be in grave danger.

Not too long ago, I was able to slip in and out of my home on Rue Miromesnil in Paris with little notice, but the horrible things

I saw haunt me. On one occasion, I met the mob on the boulevard. They paraded the street with the head and body of the unfortunate Princesse de Lamballe, an innocent victim of this insanity. As I tried to return to my country home in Meudon, south of Paris, I found all passages obstructed. I was forced to return to my home in Paris, where I had to exit my carriage and walk many blocks unescorted. On several occasions, I was compelled to duck into the shadows to hide from the patrols. Many of those on the court have been murdered. Others, should they be found, are listed by the Revolutionary government for the guillotine. Such lust for bloodletting I have never seen.

When I finally arrived home, I was exhausted and trembling so much that I thought I would faint. My servants had to carry me inside. As I was trying to regain my composure after such an ordeal, the Marquis de Champcenets, who was one of those listed for the guillotine, came to my house begging for refuge. While I'd never been terribly fond of him or his political position, I could not fathom anyone being subjected to the barbaric behavior outside in the streets. I, therefore, with trepidation and the grave possibility of being found a traitor, hid him between the mattresses of my bed. When the designated patrol of the programme of domiciliary entered my home, having been told that someone saw the Marquis enter my dwelling but not come out, they visited all rooms before entering my bedroom, even drawing their bayonets through all the servant's beds, slicing their mattresses to pieces.

Somehow I drew courage from an invisible source. When they entered my room, I feigned sickness, yet remained entirely civil and of reasonable mind, even inviting them to have wine, fine liqueurs, and cold pie. At this, they were most appreciative, though they did not avail themselves of my hospitality. After an hour of questions and threats, they left my house, bidding me a good night, as if I could enjoy any of it after such a visit. In the aftermath of their search, I almost lost my sanity from the stress. The poor Marquis was practically expired from being compressed for so long.

Unfortunately, it was necessary to harbor this wanted man for many days. Finally, I was able to exit Paris and return to Meudon with the Marquis tucked into the bottom of my coach, a most harrowing trip for both of us. Once in the country, others made arrangements to smuggle him out of

France to England. I have no idea what became of him.

I would love to steal away to London as well, but getting out of France is impossible. The Revolutionary government has forbidden anyone to leave for fear royalists will escape. They go house-to-house every week taking a census just to make sure. It's difficult for me to travel from my home in Paris to Meudon and back. Even that falls under their suspicious eyes. Oh, how I yearn for a return to sanity!

I pray this letter finds you well and Georgiana growing in your kindness. It is with great care that this communique is being sent clandestinely by a trusted friend in order to reach you. When this entire dreadful business comes to an end, I desire a visit from you and my daughter. What a wonderful distraction that will be.

With Affection,
Grace

Given the confusion of the revolution, Grace was thrilled to receive a reply, even though it took a year to reach her.

My Dearest Grace,
I am deeply saddened to learn of your hardships and wish I could do something to

make your life more bearable. I pray civility will soon return. In the meantime, allow me to speak of Georgiana.

She is growing into a fine young lady who loves her tutor and learns very quickly. I keep your portrait in the parlor so she can remember how beautiful you are. Sometimes I hear her talking to it when no one is around. Though you are spoken of often, I'm sure it's hard for her to understand why you're in France while she is here in London with me. Yet, she is loved very deeply and is never devoid of affection.

She accompanies me to the theater and loves each play. She enjoys painting, but her true love is dancing. She is light on her feet and quite rhythmical. I'm sure she will enjoy many a party when she is old enough, and the men will find her exceptional on the dance floor.

I pray that you will be well and safe. Georgiana sends her love, as do I.

> With Great Affection,
> George

Quite some time passed before Grace was able to write George again:

Dearest George,

Please forgive the length of time (almost two years) since my last letter. I'm sure you will understand why I was delayed after reading this.

As you have undoubtedly heard, King Louis XVI was beheaded. It was the bleakest day I ever saw. Even the clouds seemed to mourn and weep. People dared not to step out of their houses or look at each other. I was equally shocked and saddened to hear that the Egalite had voted against him. To make matters worse, Queen Marie Antoinette was also beheaded. It seemed even a raised eyebrow in protest was reason enough for an arrest by the revolutionaries.

With all this, the thought of returning to Paris ever again was abhorrent to me. However, I was taken ill several weeks after the King's death and needed to see a doctor. I therefore ventured into Paris with great apprehension. It was a dreary place. No movement on the streets except for a few carriages. The playhouses were filled with none but Jacobins, the most radical and ruthless of the political groups, as well as women of common status. No honest, decent inhabitants would venture out.

Thankfully, I was able to see a doctor, recover from my illness, and return to the country. Several weeks later, however, I was pressed into hiding a woman who was a cousin of a judge of the court. She came to me as a last resort believing I had connections that would somehow allow her and her children to escape the terror. Her children were sent to friends. Meanwhile, she stayed in my secret closet during searches by the patrol, both of our lives in immeasurable peril should she be discovered. It was there in the closet that she was hiding when I was first arrested.

It seems someone was out for me from the beginning, believing I was sympathetic to the royals. It became obvious they were just waiting for an opportune time to accuse me. It was after midnight when they appeared at my house. My servants were scared witless. After searching my home, they found a letter they felt supported their belief of my collusion. Having never opened the letter, it still bore the seal of the writer Mr. Fox. He had given the letter to me to carry to Mr. Humundy, but the opportunity never arose. They took all my papers and hardly allowed time for me to wrap a shawl about my shoulders, though it was most chilly. I wish I'd had on my father's ring. You know how comforting it is to me, but alas, I left so abruptly that it remained behind

— a better place, no doubt, given the anxious hands of those who arrested me.

I was taken before a tribunal and the evidence presented. The letter was opened and read. They asked me to read and interpret it, as there seemed no one in the tribunal could read English. This seemed unlikely, and I'm sure one of their compatriots was well educated in English and just waiting for me to make an error. Needless to say, as the letter was interpreted correctly and was favorable to the uprising, they could find no fault with me. Yet, the jury of men remained split as to my fate, believing I must have committed some egregious act to warrant my arrest. I was then taken to prison, where I encountered hundreds of persons whose situation was similar or worse than mine.

I was moved from one prison to another, the conditions as varied as the treatment from the guards. In one, I lived among mice and rats, both human and animal. In another, I was treated with high esteem. Regardless of my circumstances, however, I met some very lovely people who had been thrown into prison for even the most minor of offenses. Their friendship provided great comfort to me and was indeed a blessing.

Every day, the guards laughed in our faces with such cruelty and subjected us to the most debilitating promise — we would be beheaded at any moment. At one point my hair was even cut off in preparation for the guillotine. Thousands of decent people were taken to the scaffold. The horror I watched and heard will forever remain etched in my mind — piercing screams, physical struggles, heart-wrenching goodbyes. Wives and husbands were torn apart as were parents from their children. How cruel we can be to one another. My faith is all that kept me from losing hope and my mind.

In the end, I was released after a year and a half of being shuffled from one horrible prison to another without a jury finding any fault. How ironic that those who wanted change appeared to mimic those whose power they overthrew. And the Duke de Orleans? After voting to have his cousin the King put to death, he was tried for treason and beheaded.

I was finally released and am now back at Meudon. Calm is returning little by little to Paris, though it is quite a different place than it was only a short while ago. The patrols put seals on my dwelling when they arrested me, but when I returned, many of my things — furniture and personal belongings — had vanished. Yet, these were minor compared to what I retained — my life and my precious ring, which I fortunately had concealed in a special hiding place.

I wish only for peace and calmness. As soon as I am able, I will travel to London for a long-cherished visit with you and my daughter. Keep me in your prayers. I look so forward to seeing you.

With affection,

Grace

~~~

Abel turned the page. Father Albert had added a postscript in his handwriting:

In 1795, Lord Cholmondeley married heiress Charlotte Bertie from an old, powerful, and distinguished English family. She assisted in bringing up Georgiana, who subsequently married and had a daughter, Georgina After Georgiana's death at age thirty-one in 1813 from a fall during her second pregnancy, Grace returned permanently to France. After much parlaying and monies exchanged between Marchioness Bertie and Anne, the new wife of Georgiana's husband, young Georgina Cavendish-Bentinck, Grace's granddaughter, subsequently came under the care of Lord Cholmondeley and Bertie.

For the last two years of her life, Grace was a paying lodger in the home of M. Dupuis, the mayor of Ville d'Avray, where she lived off her annuities. In 1823, she received last rights and died alone at age sixty-nine from debilitating health problems she acquired during her prison stays. Lord Cholmondeley paid for her burial in the Père Lachaise Cemetery.

In Grace's will, she left the ring, her money, and a memoir to Georgina. The book, Journal of My Life during the French Revolution, was published in 1856.

~

Abel placed the book on the table. He removed his glasses, rubbed his eyes, and gazed into the fire. The glow mesmerized him as he reflected on the last chapter. Grace had lived an extraordinary life at an extraordinary time. Her decision to write a memoire piqued his interest, and he made a mental note to try to find her book in a Paris bookstore before returning to Brooklyn.

"Well, how did you find Grace's story?" Father Albert crossed the room and stood by his chair.

"Just like the others — amazing yet heartbreaking — each of them strong women in their own right, but their lives took such tragic turns."

"Just two more chapters to go. Then we'll set out on what you came here for."

Abel looked at Father Albert. "It will be a happy yet sad day."

"No doubt."

"How about I read the next chapter and then you let me treat you to lunch? I can finish the last chapter later when we return."

"Perfect, I'll leave you to your reading then."

As was his custom, Father Albert gave the sign of the cross before leaving.

Chapter 14

Julia and Winston ate lunch in a quaint little restaurant, Crêpes Savoureuses, four blocks from the hotel before heading back toward the church.

"Should we find Mr. Moody, I'm sure it will be an interesting encounter," Winston said.

"Yes, I just hope Mr. Moody is still there."

"Where else could he be?"

Julia swept her hand across the Paris landscape. "Anywhere."

"Perhaps, but from my conversation with him in the elevator, he appeared to be focused on something far more important than tourist attractions. The question is, just what kind of a *something* is it, and what does it have to do with our ring?"

"That's the million-dollar question, isn't it?" Julia said, her face and pace filled with determination.

Few words passed between them as they retraced their steps from earlier that morning down the Paris streets. Just as they passed the Babioles et Jijoux jewelry store, Masego bounded out of the door and down the sidewalk. He ran in front of Julia and Winston and faced them while flashing his palms in a gesture to stop.

"Please, perhaps I was a bit hasty before. Can we talk?" he asked, walking backward at their pace.

"What's left to say?" Winston's tone was firm as he and Julia kept their resolute strides.

"Please!" Masego grasped Julia's arm in restraint. Her turquoise tote bag fell and spilled its contents on the sidewalk.

"Oh, I'm so sorry!" Masego dropped down to pick up her things and stuff them back into her bag.

"Just what do you think you're doing?" Winston grabbed Masego by the arm and yanked him to his feet.

"Perhaps I should ask you two the same question." Masego handed the bag back to Julia — minus one important item. He turned a paper around so Julia and Winston could see it.

Julia grabbed for the paper, but Masego jerked it out of her reach.

"Well?" He waggled the printout of the ring at them. "Where did you get this?"

Julia and Winston looked at each other with dumbfounded expressions, neither knowing quite what to say.

Masego pointed at the image. "This is a picture of my ring!" he said loudly.

"No, it isn't!" Julia said in an equally loud voice. "It's a picture of *my* ring!" She grounded her feet apart and thrust her fists on her hips. She and Masego glared at each other as though in a staring contest, waiting for the other to blink.

Just then, Winston realized they were not only blocking the sidewalk, but a crowd was gathering around the vociferous trio.

"Perhaps we need to sit down and talk about this," Winston said in a calm voice. He looked from Julia to Masego with urgent expectation. Julia realized he was trying to deescalate the heated argument.

"Good idea, follow me." Masego beckoned them along as he turned back down the sidewalk.

"No!" Julia said in a panicked voice. "We don't have time. We need to find Mr. Moody!" As soon as she blurted out his name, she wished she could take it back.

Masego froze and wheeled around. "Abel Moody? The jeweler?"

Julia and Winston stared at Masego — their eyes wide, jaws slack.

"How do you know Abel Moody?" Winston asked.

Before Masego could answer, a tall, middle-aged mustachioed man in a blue uniform pushed his way through the gathered crowd. He wore a black baton on his left hip and a sidearm tucked into a black leather holster on his right. Police Nationale was embroidered above the silver badge on his breast pocket. The man looked from Julia to Winston and finally to Masego.

"*Excusez-moi. Y a-t-il des problèmes ici?*" The officer's hand rested on his firearm as he asked the trio if there was a problem.

All three looked at the officer.

"*Non,*" Masego said, "*il n'y a pas de problème ici.*" His provoking eyes and tone softened to one of conciliation as he told the officer there was no problem.

"Actually, yes, there is a problem," Julia said, her eyes and voice retaining fiery nuance.

The officer switched to English laced with a heavy French accent once he realized he was speaking to Americans.

"And monsieur, what do you say?" The officer's eyes bore down on Winston.

"No, officer, there's no problem here. We were just heading to the café to talk it out, weren't we, Julia?" Winston shot Julia a stern look.

"Well, miss, which is it? Yes or no?" The officer eyeballed Julia with an unyielding glare.

She hesitated. "Uh . . . no, there's no problem." Her tone was one of acquiescence.

"Then I suggest you move along. No need to block the walkway any further." The officer shooed them down the sidewalk with a hand gesture. Without a word, the three strode away. Julia felt the officer's eyes boring into her back until they rounded the corner.

"Here," Winston said. He shoved open the door of the Bien Café, the first one he found, and ushered Julia and Masego inside. He led them to a bistro table in a corner and ordered cappuccinos all around. "All right, let's all try to calm down now and discuss this rationally."

Julia filled her lungs with the café air – a mixture of coffee and croissants – and let it slowly escape. "Mr. Bamudy, I realize you think the ring belongs to you because of some family connection, but my grandmother gave me this ring years ago for when I became engaged."

Masego unfolded the image of the ring on the table between them.

"My great-great-great-uncle designed and fashioned this ring back in the early 1500s," he said, tapping the paper with emphasis. "He had worked as a slave in the gem mines of Tanzania for five years, faceting gems for Europe's rich. When he was finally able to escape, he made the dangerous trip to Paris and worked for a master jeweler named Louis Van Berquem. When Louis died, he left the store to my uncle. The store has been in my family ever since. Each of my uncles was a master jeweler, and they kept detailed records of every piece of jewelry they made and who they sold it to. After Mary of Burgundy's death, my uncle redesigned her original diamond ring into this one and sold it to the queen of France, Catherine de' Medici."

"I had no idea my ring had such royal history!" Julia said.

"You mean, *my* ring." Masego locked eyes with Julia in another standoff.

"With all due respect, it's not your ring," Winston said to Masego. "It belongs to Julia. It's been in her family for more than fifty years. Obviously, much longer than it has been in yours."

"Yes, well, that may be legally true, but it will always be *my* ring no matter who owns it. But back to the reason we're here. How do you know Abel Moody, and what does he have to do with the ring?"

Julia crossed her arms and leaned in on the table. "How do *you* know him?"

Masego drew air through his teeth. "I guess I won't get the answer to my question until I answer yours."

Julia titled her head as a prod for him to continue.

"Well, Abel happened into my store the other day, and we talked about the ring right here in this café. Much to our surprise, we discovered he is a distant cousin of mine from the side of the family that immigrated to the United States."

"Oh my gosh!" Julia said. "I wondered why you looked so familiar. Now I understand. You look like a younger Abel."

"Yes, the resemblance is quite clear. Abel said he knew about the ring from a sketch his father gave him but was evasive when I told him I was looking for it. Does he have the ring?" Masego looked expectantly from Julia to Winston.

"We don't know," Julia and Winston said in unison.

"Then why are you looking for him?"

Julia relayed her long relationship with Mr. Moody, how the ring came to her grandmother through her murdered relative, Louise, and how Mr. Moody had fled New York after she gave it to him to appraise and clean. She also explained it was the police who discovered he had flown to Paris.

"That's about all we know," Winston said. "We flew here to find him at his hotel, and we did. We followed him to a church not far from here. But we haven't seen him since," Winston said.

"You followed him to Eglise Catholique de Saint-Paul around the corner, and he hasn't come out?"

"Not as far as we know, but we didn't stick around. We were on our way back there when you stopped us," Julia said.

Masego sat back.

"What are you thinking?" Winston asked.

"That we can help each other find the ring."

Julia let out a mocking laugh. "Why would *I* want to help *you* find a ring you think is yours, and why would *you* want to help *me* find the same ring I *know* is mine?"

"Well, don't we both want the same thing — to find the ring?"

Winston and Julia nodded.

"Believe me, I'll make it most worthwhile for you to find the ring and return it to my family." Masego looked from Julia to Winston.

Julia sat back. "Mr. Bamudy, the ring is priceless as far as I'm concerned. Besides . . . we can't be bought." She crossed her arms over her chest.

"Really? How does one million dollars sound? And I'll throw in a replica of the ring for your engagement."

Julia sucked air, and her eyes grew wide. "The ring means *that* much to you?"

"Isn't it obvious? Oh, one other thing: I've been told the ring is cursed."

Winston turned to Julia. "I told you we shouldn't use the ring."

"Don't be ridiculous, Winston," Julia said. "Things aren't cursed. Neither are people."

"Apparently, you've never heard of the Hope Diamond curse." Masego raised his brows and looked from Winston to Julia.

"Only vaguely," Julia said with a shrug of her shoulders.

"Well, let me tell you the story. Fable or not, jewelers know it quite well, and it's one my father told me numerous times over the years." Masego leaned slightly forward and spoke in a soft, deliberate voice as if delivering a ghost story.

"Jean-Baptiste Tavernier, a diamond merchant, is said to have stolen the original one hundred fifteen-carat blue diamond in 1653 from a Hindu statue in India. The priests were so angry they put a curse on him to punish him. He died a slow and painful death after wild dogs tore him apart. After that, terrible things happened to many of the people who possessed the stone or their family members. Some even died."

Julia's and Winston's eyes appeared as large as the diamond as Masego continued.

"Of the many people who wore or owned the diamond, one of the most notable was King Louis XIV of France, who bought the diamond in 1673. All of his six legitimate children, except one, died in childhood, and he eventually died of gangrene at age seventy-six. King Louis XVI inherited the gem and gave it to his wife, Marie Antoinette. As you well know, they were both beheaded during the French Revolution.

"The diamond was stolen during the pillaging of the palace and didn't show up until two decades later when

Wilhelm Fals, a Dutch jeweler, recut the diamond. His son robbed and murdered him. Philip Hope purchased the recut diamond in 1839 and renamed it the Hope Diamond. His descendant, Lord Francis Hope, fell into financial ruin, having lived a life of indulgences. He died broke and alone after being forced to sell the diamond to pay his debts."

Masego paused for a sip of cappuccino. Julia and Winston sat like statues, waiting for the rest of the story.

"After Greek merchant Simon Maoncharides bought the diamond, he drove his car off a precipice and killed himself, his wife, and child. In 1911, American heiress Evalyn Walsh McLean bought the diamond. Her husband left her for another woman, ran their fortune into the ground, and died in a mental institution. She was forced to sell the family newspaper. I think you've heard of it, *The Washington Post?* She also lost her son and daughter — the son in an auto accident, the daughter from a drug overdose. She died shortly after her daughter. The next owner was Harry Winston, the well-known jeweler. He was told the only way to break the curse was to give the stone away. He ended up donating it to the Smithsonian Institution in 1958 after it traveled in exhibitions for ten years. It remains in Washington, D.C., to this day."

Julia inhaled deeply, as though she had been holding her breath throughout the saga. "Okay, it's all interesting, but what does it have to do with my ring?"

"Bad things seem to happen to whoever possesses the ring. Mary of Burgundy met her untimely death when her horse fell on her while wearing the ring with the original stones. Catherine de' Medici, queen of France, owned the redesigned ring using the original gems, and her husband died from internal bleeding from a jousting accident. Plus, each of her sons died shortly after taking the throne. Then there was your relative, Louise, who was murdered with her husband. I feel confident that if we knew the histories of the other women who possessed the ring along the way, we'd find that terrible things happened to them as well. I'm sure you don't want to put your marriage in jeopardy before it's even begun."

"Of course not," Julia said, an indignant expression on her face. Why would anyone think that?

Masego arched an eyebrow at the couple, his eyes like dark wells. "Well then, whether you believe in curses or not, there's one important question you need to answer: Is the ring so important you want to take that chance?"

Julia and Winston locked eyes. She believed the Hope Diamond curse was nothing but superstitious baloney, but could Winston be right? Maybe they should find another engagement ring.

"Think about my offer," Masego said.

Chapter 15

Abel sat in his chair in front of the fire and thought back to his family of jewelers who had kept the sapphire ring in the back of their minds and its sketch in their drawer. They knew the famed piece of jewelry was out there somewhere, and hoped someday it would turn up. That someday was now.

Because of the ring, he had traveled to France to understand its historic significance. He was grateful to spend time with the women who had possessed the ring and embraced their amazing, albeit tumultuous and heartbreaking, stories. Yet, now, he was coming to the end of the book. He likened it to having spent quality time with a long-lost friend — one you hoped would stick around a while so you could get to know him or her better.

Abel turned the page.

~~~

Georgina Cavendish-Bentinck

Tears rolled down Georgina's cheeks and dripped onto the bodice of her dark-blue velvet dinner dress as she slipped the sapphire ring her grandmother had left her onto her right pinky. In a few minutes, she and Mimi, her endearing name for Lady Cholmondeley, would be carried by coach to the Royal Pavilion in Brighton to dine with King William IV and Queen Adelaide.

They had traveled to the seaside town, seventy-five kilometers south of London, the day before so they could relax before the royal engagement. They would return to London tomorrow.

Dowager Marchioness of Cholmondeley pushed in her wheelchair by her maid, Dahlia, stopped in the threshold of Georgina's room when she saw her crying. "Is something wrong, dear?"

"Not really, Mimi. I've got high expectations for a festive evening, but somehow putting on the ring brought a unexpected flood of memories of my mother and grandmother." Georgina wiped the tears away with a pink hanky edged in lace.

"I know it's been hard on you. You were only two when your mother died, and I suppose our descriptions and stories of her weren't really enough for a child to hold dear. Then you lost your beloved grandmother when you were ten. And of course, Lord Cholmondeley, your most ardent champion, died just four years later. Now you choose to be my constant companion, forsaking marriage, children, and a life of your own. It's a lot to take in. Just know that I've loved you as though you were my granddaughter, my own flesh and blood."

Georgina knelt by her wheelchair. "You've given me more than I ever deserve."

Lady Cholmondeley kissed the top of Georgina's head. "Nonsense, my dear, you've been a joy to care for and a delightful companion." She circled her index finger in the air. "Now let's be off! We don't want to keep the king waiting."

Georgina, who was in her late twenties, recalled the story of how the loving Cholmondeley family had taken her infant mother into their home and brought her up as their own daughter. Lady Cholmondeley had told Georgina how thrilled they were when her mother wed, and they couldn't have been more excited when she had Georgina.

After her mother's death, Georgina's father, Lord Charles Cavendish-Bentinck, remarried. Apparently, his new wife, Anne, wasn't too keen on having an instant family and was more than happy to entertain the proposition that the Cholmondeleys take Georgina into their home, just like they had done for her mother. That is when the tug of war began — a custody battle that become, more or less, a matter of money.

From conversations with her grandmother, Georgina knew the Cholmondeleys didn't care for Anne or the fact they had to barter for custody of her like some Persian rug in a bazaar. Anne would only grant the Cholmondeleys custody in exchange for a tidy sum to be deposited into a trust for her own future children. Georgina believed in her heart of hearts that paying Anne was a decision the Cholmondeleys made in love — one they never regretted.

Still, why hadn't her father fought harder for her? Why had he allowed his new wife to dictate the forfeiture of his daily relationship with his daughter for little more than several thousand pounds? Regardless, Georgina was glad the Cholmondeleys had paid the price, and she knew they felt she was well worth every pound.

Georgina's mouth formed an O as the coach pulled onto the grounds of the Royal Pavilion.

"I've never seen anything like this, Mimi. It's magical!"

"Yes, dear, it is. And the inside is just as decorative, so I've been told."

The massive building's Indo-Islamic exterior, featuring four large domes and more than a dozen minarets, reminded Georgina of photos she had seen of Islamic mosques or Indian temples. The intricate second-floor railing and entrance archways resembled lace.

A uniformed servant led her and Mimi through the foyer and down a hallway to the sitting room, where they mingled with guests until called for dinner. The building's sheer size, architecture, and décor mesmerized her. Colorful, elaborate frescoes decorated the ceiling while portraits of British royalty hung on the walls.

The dining room in the main rotunda was much more ornate than the sitting room. The lofty round concave ceiling was painted in a lively sky blue with dark green banana leaves emanating from its center. A massive chandelier embellished with hand-blown colored glass, equally as opulent and colorful as the room's décor, dangled from the center of the rotunda's ceiling above the dining table.

Six floor-to-ceiling double windows were scalloped across the top in dark orange velvet drapes that matched the accent color of the walls painted the same blue as the ceiling. Life-sized portraits of other British royalty in elaborate gilded frames adorned the walls. A long banquet table with three dozen seats stood in the middle of the room. At one end was a sizeable dance floor of inlaid wood. A black grand piano dominated a corner.

Spending the evening with the king and queen was as enchanting as Georgina had expected — the food, the drink, the dancing. The fact that she sat next to the queen while savoring Cornish game hens stuffed with wild rice and mushrooms made the occasion even more extraordinary! And while she had anticipated a stuffy affair, she was shocked by its informality. Even though the king was twenty-five years older than the queen, both proved quite unpretentious, putting their guests at ease by effortlessly mingling and dancing with as many as possible.

Back in her hotel room, Georgina analyzed her plump form as she brushed out her long brown hair in front of the full-length mirror in her nightclothes. She didn't have the slim figure her grandmother and mother had at her age, nor was her appetite as dainty. Yes, she enjoyed food, particularly breads and pastries, and it showed.

She moved closer to the mirror to inspect her face. Although she had her mother's eyes and nose, she had to admit her facial features weren't as attractive as that of either her mother or grandmother. Rather than heart shaped, her face was rounder with full cheeks, a generous chin, and a short, thick neck. She'd been that way since childhood, actually. Everyone said she'd outgrow it. Well, she hadn't. Her baby fat had proved stubborn, shadowing her from childhood into adolescence. That was why, Georgina mused, that her classmates had nicknamed her Hippo. They had couched it as an endearing name, but she knew better, of course. Now as an adult, her hefty figure endured, unfortunately.

Throughout her life, that name and her ample figure had made her self-conscious and contributed to her desire to remain celibate and maintain indifference toward suitors, though several showed sincere interest. Yet, she wasn't lonely. She enjoyed plenty of social life with Mimi, and both of them loved the theater.

After returning to London, Georgina and Mimi attended one of their favorite productions, *The Beggar's Opera,* a ballad opera in which John Gay rewrote the lyrics of popular songs in a humorous and satirical way.

Unfortunately, the unexpected occurred a few weeks later during the intermission of *The London Merchant*.

"Someone help!" Georgina yelled. She knelt by Mimi's wheelchair in their elevated box, patted her hand, and fanned her face with a hand painted Baroque fan. Tears tumbled down Georgina's cheeks when the touch of Mimi's lifeless body became shocking reality. She caressed Mimi's pallid face and whispered in her ear, "Mimi, you can't leave me."

At seventy-three, however, Mimi had left Georgina, who was not yet thirty.

In the barrister's office, Georgina learned that Lady Cholmondeley's will provided handsomely for her, but the house and furniture were to be sold along with other personal effects and the proceeds divided among Lady Cholmondeley's sisters. Before the sale, however, Georgina was to select two dozen items of which she was especially fond — jewelry, oil paintings, gifts from the royal family, furnishings, accessories, and the like. With her inheritance, she would be able to purchase and furnish an apartment and cover living expenses. The money would last twenty-five years if she was prudent.

The bequest was most appreciated, but it meant Georgina would have to manage her own finances for the first time. This scared and intimidated her. It also meant she would have to muster the courage to venture out on her own, something she was most apprehensive to do. Her entire life had centered around the Cholmondeley family and their acquaintances. Now, she would have to reach out herself to maintain those friendships if she wanted to be invited to dinners or parties. She felt awkward, uncomfortable.

Within a year, Georgina's social life in London had dwindled to nothing except for attending the theater alone, which she still adored. She bought tickets to every production in London, even seeing some plays multiple times. She became so immersed in the stories that she memorized the lines and recited them at night in front of her mirror as though she was the one on stage. Through her frequent attendance and generous support, she became known to many of the actors, directors, and producers. She even traveled to France to see productions deemed worthwhile and rented an apartment so she could attend the theater often.

As Georgina stepped into middle age, she became especially fond of a new French actress, Sarah Bernhardt, who was spreading her wings on the big stage. Georgina enjoyed the emerging thespian in several minor productions. Later, she made sure to be among the first to purchase a ticket when Sarah played the title role in *Iphigénie,* a dramatic tragedy written by French playwright Jean Racine. The premiere, however, proved disastrous for the young performer when she suffered stage fright and rushed her lines.

Francisque Sarcey, a most influential theater critic, reviewed Sarah's performance in *L'Opinion Nationale*: ". . . she carries herself well and pronounces with perfect precision. That is all that can be said about her at the moment."

It was a scathing review, and Georgina, now forty, felt so sorry for the eighteen-year-old actress that she invited her to tea to lend her emotional support. Although both women knew of each other, they had never been formally introduced. Georgina easily spotted Sarah as she entered the Hazlitt hotel restaurant where they had decided to meet. Her thin frame, head of long, frizzy brown hair, and bohemian attire were hard to miss. The two women embraced as though they were family friends. They ordered tea and pastries and engaged in small talk until the refreshments arrived.

"I've attended all your performances and am truly impressed with your potential. It must be so exciting to be on stage! Do tell me what it's like." Georgina, who spoke in French, which she learned from her grandmother and time spent in France, leaned forward, eager to absorb every word the young actress had to say.

"Well, it is exciting. Being able to interpret the thoughts of the playwright, performing in front of an audience, and interacting with other actors is a thrilling and exhilarating experience. Except, of course, when you perform badly and receive reviews like the one Monsieur Sarcey wrote. Then you want to crawl into a rabbit hole and never come out." Sarah's shoulders drooped, her gaze turned downward, and a slight pout puckered her lips.

"Yes, I can understand that." Georgina wanted to be as empathetic as possible. "But you must view that performance as only a minor hiccup in your developing career. I wouldn't be surprised if you show all of them just how magnificent you are not too long from now. I predict

Monsieur Sarcey will soon eat his words served in a tart dish of humble pie." Georgina let out a modest laugh and gave Sarah a broad smile.

"Your words are so kind and your encouragement most refreshing. I certainly hope they are true." Sarah took a bite of her fruit pastry.

"They are, mark them. You have been blessed with a rare talent. Just give it time."

"You know, Mademoiselle Bentinck, you and I have more in common than the theater."

"Do we?"

"Yes. You see, my mother met your grandmother, Mademoiselle Dalrymple, toward the end of her life. My mother is in the same profession."

Sarah leaned in with wide eyes and spoke in a whisper. "Your mother is a courtesan?"

"Yes. I am the offspring of one of her relationships, in fact. But unlike your mother who was born of a prince who subsequently became king, I never knew who my father was."

Georgina winced. She was aware her grandmother still had a posthumous reputation in France, but didn't realize how widely known her mother's birthright was. Although she knew Sarah meant no harm by comparing their common heritage, still, it stung.

"I see," Georgina said. "Well, the good thing is your education and training has produced a first-class actress — one that the world soon will recognize."

"If I may be so bold, your ring is just lovely." Sarah pointed at the blue sapphire ring on Georgina's hand. "I notice it has little images between the gems. What do they symbolize?"

Georgina gazed at the ring, twisting it about her finger. "I'm really not sure. Speaking of my grandmother, she bequeathed it to me. Her father — my great-grandfather — gave it to her. It was quite precious to my grandmother, and I wear it to remind me of her. She was one of my devoted champions."

"It is comforting to know I have such a champion in you." Sarah gently squeezed Georgina's hand.

"Everyone needs a champion. Your career is just beginning." Georgina patted Sarah's hand.

At the end of their tea, the two women promised to stay in touch.

For the next year, Georgina stayed in France and continued to follow Sarah's career. They communicated regularly and saw each other when Sarah's schedule permitted. With no one else in her life, Georgina became absorbed with Sarah. She and the theater became of utmost importance — in essence, her lifeline to the world.

Living in Paris and retaining her apartment in London eventually became an overwhelming financial burden, one that shrunk Georgina's inheritance to a frightfully meager reserve. This forced her to return to London, where she sold some of her possessions to be able to maintain the household, pay her two servants, put food on the table, and keep a cushion. How long would it last, though?

Through their continued correspondence, Georgina stayed abreast of Sarah's tumultuous climb up the ladder of theatrical success and her life on and off the stage, including the birth of her out-of-wedlock son, Maurice. She also read the British papers that covered Sarah's professional and personal life, as well as French newspapers sent to her in London.

She kept the letters safe in a locked wooden chest in her bedroom. Newspaper articles on Sarah's performances, reviews from the critics, and mention of every new leading man — who also became her lover — stacked up in the corner of one of her closets. Years' worth of papers in the first closet turned dark ochre and brittle, while others started filling a second closet. So enamored with Sarah's theatrical fame, Georgina couldn't bring herself to part with any of them. She devoured every letter from Sarah with fervor, often pulling out old letters and reading them over and over until the paper's crispness drooped to limp pulp.

May 3, 1879

My Dear Georgina,

My life is a whirlwind. I hardly have time to breathe, but with your encouragement and that of the audience, I persevere. Things are improving now that I have negotiated a salary plus a percentage of income from the theater. Yet, I've just been told that Comédie-Française, where I perform, needs renovation, and we can't hold performances while the work is being done. Therefore, the theater company will travel to London during the renovation to present plays. I will give private performances in the homes of wealthy Londoners, and on opening night, I'm scheduled to perform the lead in one act of *Phèdre,* a French dramatic tragedy based upon Greek mythology.

Everything in my life is going well, except for my relationship with my son, Maurice. We argue often, as his indulgence in gambling often drains me of cash even though I give him a generous allowance. But how can I say no to my only child? I pray someday he will see the error of his ways.

I look forward to seeing you when in London. Pray for my success.

Sincerely,

Sarah

Now sixty-eight, Georgina used a cane, and visited with Sarah after *Phèdre* only long enough to extend an invitation for tea at her apartment the next day.

"Your performance . . . was a triumph, my dear," Georgina said in gasps as though she couldn't get enough oxygen. "You captivated . . . the entire audience with your voice . . . and gestures. Why, Sir George Arthur wrote . . . in this morning's paper . . . that you, '. . . set every nerve . . . and fiber in their bodies . . . throbbing. . . and held them spellbound.'" Georgina beamed a big smile as she held up the paper for Sarah to see it.

"Well, truth be told, I suffered a terrible case of stage fright just before I went on," Sarah said in sheepish fashion. "My voice became pitched too high, and I was perplexed as how to lower it. I also was concerned the audience would not understand Racine's classical French."

"Nonsense . . .You could have spoken Greek. . . and they would have loved you . . .You were magnificent, a total success."

After Sarah returned to France, Georgina continued to follow her career and her tours to London and then on to America. Her closet count of floor to ceiling newspapers had burgeoned to four.

One day, Georgina's maid Ellen approached her in the living room dressed in her crisp uniform, hands clasped respectfully in front of her. "Mademoiselle Bentinck, please allow Robert and me to find another place for your papers. They have displaced clothes, linens, and other items that we usually tuck out of sight. We've had to pile these in the adjoining rooms, and they are becoming unsightly and even dangerous trying to walk around them. Please, couldn't we move them to a better place?" Below her white muslin cap, a lined brow and blue eyes pleaded for resolve.

"Whose house is this?" Georgina said in a patronizing tone, as though trying to control her anger.

"Yours, of course, mademoiselle."

"And who pays . . . your salary?"

"You do."

"Then . . . if I pay your salary . . . and this is my house . . . shouldn't I have the last say . . . as to what happens inside it?" Georgina arched a brow at Ellen.

"Mademoiselle, I'm only trying to help. The piles are becoming quite tall and are attracting silver fish."

"Then kill the pests! Don't disturb the papers! They will stay in the closets . . . and I don't want to hear . . . another word about it! You will . . . just have to maneuver around the piles . . . the best you can."

Ellen, who was caught off guard by Georgina's outburst, gave her employer a slight nod before rushing from the room.

During the next four years, Georgina's life became further isolated by her failing health. Eventually, she never left the apartment, not even for the theater, but she continued to relish letters from Sarah. As the actress's career continued to rise, however, these diminished to a trickle until they stopped altogether. Without any word from Sarah, Georgina discovered in the morning news that she had come to London and secretly married the handsome Greek diplomat and known womanizer, Jacques Damala.

Georgina regarded Sarah's snub of not contacting her while in London and not even mentioning her relationship a hard slap in the face. Yet it didn't stop her obsession with Sarah. Her contact with the outside world shriveled to only her staff and newspapers carrying word of Sarah and her career, along with her limp old letters that Georgina consumed daily until they were almost shredded.

She sought refuge in her bed and rarely left her darkened room, where she kept the shades pulled even during the day. Her once elegant furnishings and dark pink silk curtains soon faded with dust since she wouldn't let Ellen clean her room.

On the afternoon of September 12, 1883, Georgina sat up in bed and selected one of the newspapers Ellen had stacked in a chair beside her bed. Her thin, trembling hands opened it to a photograph and article about Sarah and spread it over her with great care.

She lifted another.

Then another.

Soon, the opened papers resembled a black-and-white patchwork quilt that covered her from head to toe.

With a smile of satisfaction, she rested her head on the pillow. Clutching a dozen of Sarah's letters in her hands, Georgina closed her eyes for the last time.

~~~

Abel put down the book, stood, and stretched his frame. It deeply saddened him that Georgina had lived an unproductive life and died alone racked by obsession for Sarah. If nothing else, she could have offered her love of the theater to the community, especially to children who could have benefited a great deal from her knowledge and passion for the stage.

The gnawing ache in Abel's stomach reminded him how hungry he was. He grabbed his jacket and cane and left the library to find Father Albert. He wasn't in the kitchen, so Abel walked to the office. He poked his head in and found the priest dressed in street clothes behind his desk writing a letter.

"Ready for lunch?" he asked.

"Most certainly," Father Albert said. He rose from the chair, crossed the room, and lifted his jacket from the coat rack.

"This last chapter was quite gloomy, so let's find a little restaurant where we can enjoy a nice lunch with uplifting conversation."

"I know just the spot not far from here. And remember, you're paying." Father Albert chuckled.

Abel let out a hearty laugh. "You don't forget a thing, do you?"

"Not when it comes to my wallet." The priest patted his hip pocket.

Chapter 16

After leaving Masego, Julia and Winston continued their trek down the sidewalks of Paris toward the church.

"Do you know what you'll say to Mr. Moody once we find him?" Winston asked.

"I'll want to know where the ring is."

"Are you still thinking you want the ring back, even after everything Masego said?"

Julia stopped. "You don't really believe the ring is cursed, do you?" She looked at Winston, a question mark engraved in her expression.

Winston hesitated. "Honestly, I don't know, Julia. The thing is, even if it isn't, do you want to wear a ring knowing it was worn by several women who died tragically while it was in their possession, including your relative, Louise? If something should happen during our engagement or marriage, wouldn't we wonder if it was because of a natural part of life or the so-called curse?"

Julia hesitated. "Well, I must admit, it's something to consider. But I always thought of you as a savvy entrepreneur, someone who knows his own mind, has a clear vision, and is not bothered by what others think. I mean, you own your own app company, Winston, and you went through a lot just to open the doors. If you'd listened to what people said about a start-up with all the competition, financial burdens, and other difficulties, you'd never even gotten off the ground."

Without warning, Winston pulled Julia through a door of a shoe emporium.

"Looking for Berluti or Bruno Magli?" Julia asked, surprised.

"Shhh." Winston brought his index finger to his lips and then pointed at the sidewalk through the window. Mr. Moody and another man walked by deep in conversation.

"Let's go!" Julia bolted for the door.

"Wait!" Winston pulled her back. "We can't just pop up and confront him on the sidewalk. This needs to be nonchalant, something coincidental."

Julia and Winston crept out the door. They followed Mr. Moody and the man two blocks until they entered Le Bistro. Through the large front window they could see the hostess seat them next to a back wall. Fortunately, there was an empty table next to them. Julia and Winston looked at each other in silent agreement and entered the restaurant.

Julia sat with her back to Mr. Moody while Winston faced the man who sat opposite the jeweler. It was perfect — they could overhear their conversation, yet not be recognized.

As Julia and Winston ate their salmon over asparagus in silence, the mundane conversation between the unknown man and Mr. Moody — a bit of history mixed with memories from each of their childhoods and current events — didn't reveal anything about the ring. It wasn't until Mr. Moody stood up after the meal that he turned around and saw Winston.

"Hello, we meet again," he said to Winston. "Find the interesting, out-of-the-way attractions you were looking for?" Mr. Moody glanced over at Julia. "Why, Miss Julia! What are you doing here?"

"Mr. Moody!" Julia arose and gave Mr. Moody a perfunctory hug. "I'm so surprised to see you! This is my fiancé, Winston." Winston stood too.

Mr. Moody's eyes were wide with wonder. "The man I met in the elevator."

"One and the same," Winston said.

"And I'm Father Albert." The priest stepped alongside Mr. Moody to meet the couple and hugged each of them.

"What are you doing here?" Mr. Moody asked, looking from Julia to Winston.

"Actually, we were looking for you, Mr. Moody," Julia said. "Your store was all locked up, and we became even more worried when you didn't return my calls. We were so concerned that we even went to the police to make sure nothing had happened to you. They were the ones who told us you had flown to Paris."

Mr. Moody gave Julia a second hug. "As you can see, I'm fine, Miss Julia. There's no need to worry."

"Why did you leave so abruptly, Mr. Moody? And why Paris?" Julia's eyes welled with tears and spilled down her cheeks.

Mr. Moody framed her face with his hands and brushed them away with his thumbs.

"Actually, he came to see me," Father Albert said before Mr. Moody could answer. "You see, I knew his father and thought perhaps Mr. Moody would enjoy some time away to reminisce."

"I wasn't planning to be gone very long, maybe a week at the most," Mr. Moody said. "I didn't mean to upset anyone."

"And our ring?" Julia asked.

Mr. Moody squeezed Julia's hand. "The ring is safe, and I'll be back soon. There's no need to worry."

"I promise not to keep him much longer. He should be back in Brooklyn within the week." Father Albert looked at his watch and then at Mr. Moody. "I'm so sorry we can't talk longer, but Abel and I must go if we're going to make our appointment." He handed Winston a business card from his right pant pocket. "Please, come by the church before you leave, and we can talk more. It was nice meeting you. Father Albert nodded at the couple.

"I'm sorry, Miss Julia, but I really must go. I'll call you when I get back to Brooklyn." He gave her a hug and peck on the cheek before shaking Winston's hand. "Believe me, everything is fine." He grabbed his cane from the chair, and he and Father Albert walked toward the door.

"Well, that went well." Winston said in a sarcastic tone as his eyes followed the backs of the departing men.

"We still know nothing about our ring." He and Julia paid their bill and strolled down the street toward the hotel.

"Look, Mr. Moody is the most honest person I know. If he says not to worry, I believe him," Julia said.

"I think there's more to this than what either of them said. Besides, Mr. Moody never really said he had the ring. It was almost as though he was guilty by omission."

Julia stopped and faced Winston. "It's funny you should say that. Mr. Moody and I had a discussion one time about that very topic."

"What happened?"

"I was about to turn thirteen and had recently discovered boys. One Saturday morning, Mr. Moody saw me standing outside his shop. He had just opened the doors."

***

1999, Moody Jewelry & Repair

"Why, hello, Miss Julia. What brings you here today?" Mr. Moody stood in the doorway looking at the young girl. While her frame was still petite, she was taller, and her long hair had been cut into an attractive shoulder-length style. Her eyes were still as green as ever, though they looked a bit sad.

"Hi, Mr. Moody. I need to buy a gift for my mother." Julia forced a smile.

"Birthday?"

"No."

"Another special occasion?"

"Not exactly," Julia said rather sheepishly.

"Well, how about you come in, and we can talk about just the right gift."

Julia knew she couldn't afford anything in his store, yet she stepped inside as Mr. Moody opened the door.

"Now, what did you have in mind?"

"I'm not really sure." Julia walked to the end of the counter and perused the sparkling jewelry inside the display cases, dragging her fingers along the glass.

"I haven't seen you in a while, Miss Julia."

"School."

"I suppose it keeps you very busy."

"Very." Periodically, Julia paused to linger over a certain piece.

"See anything you like?"

"Not really," she said without looking up. She was almost at the end of the cases.

"Do you want to tell me why you're really here?" Mr. Moody asked in a soft, caring voice.

Julia turned to face him. "I did something awful, Mr. Moody, and I don't know how to fix it." Tears started rolling down her flushed cheeks in rivulets. Mr. Moody stepped behind his jewelry cases and brought back a fistful of tissues for her.

"Want to talk about it?" He ushered Julia to a chair and moved another one to sit opposite her. "Now what's this all about?"

"I told my mother I was going to a friend's house for a sleepover, but I really went to a movie with this boy from my neighborhood and then we hung out at the mall. He's fifteen, and my mother had told me I was too young to date and she didn't want me seeing him. Well, she called my friend's house that night to check on me, and my friend covered for me and told her I was in the bathroom because I hadn't gotten to her house yet. But another mother saw me at the mall. She called my mother this morning to let her know. My mother just called my friend's house and told me to come right home."

"So now you have to go home and face the fact that you lied to your mother and had someone else lie to her too?"

"Yes." Julia cried even harder. "What should I do?"

"First, I'm going to phone your mother and let her know you're here, safe, and will be home soon. Then we can keep talking." Mr. Moody ducked into the back of his shop and returned a few moments later.

"How did she sound?" Julia's eyes were wide.

"How should she sound?"

"Angry, I guess."

"That about covers it. But she said it's okay if we talk for a bit before you go home."

"I'm so sorry, Mr. Moody."

"Sorry you disobeyed your mother? Sorry you lied? Or sorry you got caught?"

Julia thought a moment. "All of the above, I guess." She blew her nose into a tissue.

"Miss Julia, let me tell you a story. When I was about your age, I wanted a new bike real bad. I already had one, but it was old and the chain kept coming off and catching in my pants cuff. I had saved and saved for a year and had almost all I needed except for five dollars. Well, this boy came by one day and wanted to buy my old bike. I told him it was a good bike but didn't mention the chain problem. I was just about to put his five dollars into my pocket when my father came out. He said, 'Oh, you're selling your bike? I'm surprised he wants it with the chain coming off.'

"I was mortified. The boy looked at me with disgust, snatched his money back, and left. I never forgot the look on his face. You see, in that moment, I'd sullied my word and my reputation. The kids in the neighborhood heard about it, and they called me Greedy Moody for a long time. I had to work hard to earn their trust back. I never forgot that lesson."

"But you didn't lie; you just didn't tell him the whole story," Julia said.

"What I did is called guilt by omission because I left out something very important. It's actually just as bad as an outright lie."

"But I lied to my mother, not some other kid."

"A lie is a lie no matter who you tell it to. The problem with lying is that it's hard to stop. Before long, another lie has to cover the first one. And then you have to cover that one with another one. Even though no one may know the truth, those lies become a huge weight that hangs around your head and your heart. When people eventually discover that you lied, your word becomes of no value, not to mention you've damaged the trust and respect others had for you."

"So what happens now?" Julia looked at Mr. Moody with wet red eyes.

"Of course, you'll have to apologize to your mother and pay the consequences. That will be whatever she deems appropriate punishment. But there is an upside to this."

"What's that?"

"A learning experience. Life is full of them."

Julia gave Mr. Moody a big hug and made her way slowly to the door. She glanced back one last time with a trembling smile.

***

"So what happened when you got home?" Winston asked. They were finally at the hotel, and he opened the lobby door for Julia.

"I was grounded for two weeks. I couldn't go to the big school dance or Cheryl's annual sleepover that all the girls went to. I certainly learned my lesson, and that was the last time I lied to my mother. Fact is, Mom and I became the best of friends after that, so there really was an upside."

"Well, now that we've found Mr. Moody, we can enjoy the rest of our six days here and see all the things we wanted to see. I've accumulated a lot of pamphlets now, you can have your pick of attractions." Winston chuckled and squeezed Julia's hand.

Julia walked to the elevator alongside Winston quite content until she remembered something. "Oh my gosh, Winston! We forgot all about Masego. What if he's still looking for the ring?" Julia pinched her face as she stared at him.

"Once we get back to New York and actually have the ring in our hands, you can decide what you want to do with it. You can either use it for our engagement or sell it to Masego. It's your ring. It's your decision."

Julia kissed Winston on the cheek. "Sounds like a plan."

Chapter 17

Father Albert and Abel headed down the sidewalk toward the church.

"I had no idea Julia and Winston were here." Abel kept his eyes focused ahead of him. "He was in the elevator with me at the hotel a couple days ago, but I didn't know who he was because I'd never met him before. Strange they are staying at the same hotel."

"No, it's not strange because they've been looking for you. What a drastic step to fly all the way here across the Atlantic! I can't imagine how shocked you must have been to see them. Obviously, there's more going on here than they're letting on."

"You mean guilt by omission?" Just as Abel uttered those words, he flashed back to his discussion with Julia so many years ago. "You know, Father, it just dawned on me that I did the same thing to Julia. I didn't lie to her about the ring, but I didn't tell her the whole truth either. I guess that makes me guilty by omission too."

"The truth will be revealed in due time, and I'm sure Julia will understand why you didn't tell her everything. Let's just get back to the church so you can read the final chapter. Then it will be time for us to complete our mission."

By the time they returned to the library, the fire had gone out. Father Albert stayed just long enough to rekindle it into a steady burn before leaving Abel to finish the book.

Toasty by the fire, Abel wondered what he would encounter with the last woman.

~~~

Sarah Bernhardt

"Madame, where would you like the boxes?"

The uniformed delivery boy stood respectfully on the landing with a line of at least ten other boys behind him each holding a large box. He stared wide-eyed at the middle-aged woman in front of him in her flowing flowered silk ensemble.

"What is this?" asked Sarah, who had been called to the door by her maid, Giselle.

"A delivery from Mademoiselle Georgina Cavendish-Bentinck of London." The pack leader handed Sarah a manifest — twenty large boxes and one small one.

"Put them here." Sarah pointed at her foyer and made way for the infantry.

"Here's the last box." The leader handed Sarah a much smaller package along with a letter. "I was told to make sure I delivered these to you in person. Can you please sign the delivery slip?"

She obliged and rewarded him with a handsome tip.

"Giselle, please bring me some scissors. I can't imagine what Georgina has sent me."

"Yes, madame." Giselle retrieved a pair of long scissors from the kitchen. She proceeded to slice the string and remove the brown wrapping paper from the first box.

Sarah opened it. Nothing but old, discolored newspapers. The second box yielded the same result. The third box contained the letters she had written to Georgina. Was this a mistake? A joke?

Sarah thrust her hands on her hips, perplexed by the boxes.

"She kept all these newspapers and my letters. Why?" Sarah asked.

"Perhaps the letter and smaller box contain an explanation," Giselle said.

"Perhaps." Sarah walked into the study, grabbed a letter opener from the desk and sliced open the envelope.

January 12, 1894

Dear Mademoiselle Bernhardt,

Mademoiselle Georgina Cavendish-Bentinck passed away on September 12,

1883. As she had many debts, they were paid by selling her personal belongings at auction, all except the items in these boxes. These were stipulated in her will to go to you.

As you know, she followed your career from its inception and kept every paper that mentioned you and your rise to fame. With no heirs, Mademoiselle Cavendish-Bentinck wanted you to have these papers chronicling your life. As well, she left you something very special. You will find it in the smaller box. It is to thank you for your friendship and allowing her glimpses of your life through your correspondence.

If you have any questions, please contact me.

With regards,
Reginald Farnsworth, solicitor
for Georgina Cavendish-
Bentinck

Sarah sat on a thick upholstered chair and opened the smaller box. Honestly, why would Georgina send her anything after their relationship had dwindled to nothing? In fact, Sarah felt quite unworthy after the way she had cast off Georgina the past three years.

As she picked among the crumpled newspapers used as insulation, she noticed a small blue velvet box. She let out a loud gasp when she opened the hinged lid.

"What is it?" Giselle asked, fidgeting in front of her employer. Sarah turned the box toward her to reveal the blue sapphire ring. "Oh my, how beautiful!"

Sarah hugged the box to her chest. "Ooh, Georgina's grandmother gave this to her. She cherished this ring. I remember remarking how lovely it was the first time we went to tea."

Sarah lifted the ring from its box and slid it onto the ring finger of her right hand. It was too big, of course, but she would have it resized.

That night before going to bed, Sarah slipped on the ring again and lugged in one of the boxes from the foyer. My, was it heavy! She snuggled up on her favorite turquoise chaise lounge and began combing through the newspapers. They reported the loving and contentious relationship she had with her husband, Jacques Damala.

The first article dated March 19, 1882, began with Sarah calling Jacques "the handsomest man in Europe." The second article reported their marriage in London less than a month later on April 4. An article from December of that year reviewed her role in *Fedora*, a melodrama written for her by Victorien Sardou. The play was the first time her husband had played the male lead in one of her plays. Critic Maurice Baring wrote of Sarah's performance, "a secret atmosphere emanated from her, an aroma, an attraction, which was at once exotic and cerebral . . . She literally hypnotized her audience. Was it because she was playing opposite her true love?"

Other articles reported Damala's friends calling him "Diplomat Apollo," indicating he was dangerous. Not only did he have a reputation for being a "womanizer of the high circles" and "merciless heartbreaker," but he also had a passion for morphine.

Sarah admitted she knew all of these things before she married him, including the fact he had sired an illegitimate child, but it hadn't mattered. Jacques, eleven years her junior, had mesmerized her as no man had when she met the Greek diplomat in Paris. Within weeks, she had persuaded him to give up his diplomatic post and become her lover and an actor in her company. She even remembered telling a newspaper reporter, "This ancient Greek god is the man of my dreams."

As Sarah read one article after another about their relationship, a wry smile spread across her lips as she recalled what had whetted her desire for him in the first place — he was untamable. Prior to him, she had prided herself on her ability to conquer a man, any man, and reduce him to a slave. Yet, she became exasperated when Jacques didn't submit. She sunk into frustration and emptiness when he didn't change his lifestyle after their marriage despite her money, reputation, or passion for him. She found herself at odds with him on every level, and the two fought constantly, even hurling insults at each other in public. Their marriage soon became fodder for the daily newspapers. Satirical caricatures of them flooded the tabloids for months.

Aha! There was one of those drawings just as she turned the page of the newspaper in her lap! It depicted her as a puppet master manipulating Jacques like a marionette on strings. She tossed her head back with a raucous laugh and scoffed at its implication — so preposterous now. The reality? Jacques was in North Africa after abruptly leaving her when she refused to cover any more of his expenses for women or drugs.

She rested her head against the back of the lounge and reflected on the first time Jacques left — a mere three weeks into their marriage. He had insisted she change her stage name to Sarah Damala to "honor" him. When she refused, he walked out. She didn't hear from him for three days. She was so worried! When she finally received word of him being spotted with a young Norwegian girl, she was relieved but furious. However, she took him back with open arms in an attempt to heal their quarrelsome relationship. It wasn't long, though, before he disappeared a second time. Sarah couldn't recall the catalyst for that argument, but he took off for Brussels where, once again, he enjoyed the company of prostitutes.

Sarah shook her head at herself, remembering how angry, yet desperate, she became when he was gone. What a fool she had been to take him back a second time! It was after his second homecoming that a reporter had asked why she had married him. Her defiant response? "It was the only thing I hadn't experienced."

Jacque's desertion this time, however, had been quite different, and Sarah decided it was the final straw after just eight months of marriage. She formally separated from him and moved on to a new production and lover, playwright Jean Richepin. She knew he wasn't the antidote to her estranged relationship with Jacques and that he would, most likely, only be one more in a string of lovers she charmed. For the moment, though, he would do. She adored being in a relationship, as sorted and unfulfilling as they were, and never felt content unless she had a man by her side — albeit one she could manipulate. Indeed, Jean filled that role.

Sarah likened her professional and personal life to manic depression with extreme highs and lows. Her financial chasms, which seemed to arise every three to four years, were so severe that she had to sell her carriages, horses, homes, menagerie of animals — lions, snakes, owls, and other exotic pets she collected from her trips abroad — and start all over. Then she typically ventured on world tours to replenish her finances. She performed all over Europe and in such countries as New Zealand, Samoa, Russian Empire, and Australia, sometimes for as long as two years.

Of her roller-coaster life, she recalled telling the papers: "I passionately love this life of adventures. I detest knowing in advance what they are going to serve at my dinner, and I detest a hundred thousand times more knowing what will happen to me, for better or worse. I adore the unexpected."

She closed the paper and tossed it back into the box. She would look at the others when she returned from her tour. She needed a good night's sleep because she was leaving with Giselle in the morning for South America. It was June, and every summer she closed her Sarah Bernhardt Theater, where she performed. That meant she was ready to embark on her 1892 tour.

Sarah had a custom of completing all her transactions in cash, as well as being paid in the same manner. This caused her to always carry a trunk of currency on her tours. In addition, she traveled with forty-five costume crates for her fifteen productions. Another seventy-five crates contained her off-stage clothing, two hundred and fifty pairs of shoes, sheets, tablecloths, five pillows, cosmetics, perfumes, makeup, and jewelry, which would now include the blue sapphire ring that she intended to wear off stage.

"Rio de Janeiro has been grand, don't you think, Giselle?" Sarah preened in front of the mirror in her dressing room at Theatro Municipal, where she applied a final pat of powder to her cheeks.

"Oh, yes. It's too bad this is your final act of the last show. The theater and audiences have been wonderful." In preparation for Sarah's last appearance as Floria Tosca in the melodrama *La Tosca*, Giselle smoothed creases from a floral dress on the rack. A wide red belt topped with a large pink bow would be wrapped about her waist.

"I agree. I can't believe it's time to return to France. And it will be a while before we produce this play again, even though it's one I adore."

"Madame, are you ready? Is everything in place?"

It amused Sarah that Giselle always fretted over her dramatic death scene, worried she would get hurt.

"Of course, I'm ready. As for everything else, I can only trust the stage hands have done their jobs and positioned the mattress correctly." Sarah had spoken with Adolpho, the stage manager, who assured her the cushions were positioned for her theatrical leap.

"Very good, madame. I will wait here in the dressing room until the play is over."

Sarah slipped into her dress and took a parting look in the mirror before stepping onto the Rio De Janeiro stage one last time.

TOSCA
[Who is there to witness the execution of her lover, Mario Cavaradossi]

How long is this waiting! Why are they still delaying? The sun already rises. Why are they still delaying? It is only a comedy, a fake execution but this anguish seems to last forever!
(The officer and the sergeant marshal the firing squad of soldiers before the wall and impart their instructions.)

There! They are taking aim! How handsome my Mario is!
(The officer lowers his sabre, the platoon fires and Mario Cavaradossi falls.)

There! Die! Ah, what an actor!
(The sergeant goes up to examine Cavaradossi. Spoletta (who is in on the ruse) also approaches to prevent the sergeant from delivering the coup de grace, and he covers Cavaradossi with a cloak. The officer realigns the soldiers. The sergeant withdraws the sentinel from his post at the rear, and Spoletta [henchman for Scarpia who agreed to

*Cavaradossi's fake execution in exchange for
Tosca's giving of herself to him] leads the group off
by the stairway. Tosca follows this scene with the
utmost agitation, fearing Cavaradossi may lose
patience and move or speak before the proper
moment. In a hushed voice, she warns him:)*

Oh Mario, do not move...They're going now. Be still.
They are going down...
*(Seeing the platform deserted, she goes to
listen at the stairhead. She stands there for a
moment in fear and trepidation as she thinks she
hears the soldiers returning. Again in a low voice,
Tosca warns Cavaradossi:)*

Not yet, you mustn't move...
*(She listens: they have all gone. She runs
toward Cavaradossi.)*

Quickly! Up, Mario! Mario! Up! Quickly. Come.
Up!
Up!
*(She kneels and quickly removes the cloak
and leaps to her feet, pale and terrified.)*

Mario! Mario! Dead! Dead!
*(Sobbing, she throws herself on
Cavaradossi's body.)*

Oh Mario, dead? You? Like this? Dead like this?
*(From the courtyard below the parapet and
from the narrow stairway come the confused voices
of Spoletta, Sciarrone and the soldiers. They draw
nearer.)*

CONFUSED VOICES
Scarpia stabbed? *[Tosca had stabbed him when he
tried to embrace her.]*

SCIARRONE
Yes, stabbed, I tell you!

CONFUSED VOICES
The woman is Tosca! Don't let her escape. Keep an
eye on the way out via the stairs!
*(Spoletta rushes in from the stairway, and
behind him Sciarrone shouting and waving at
Tosca.)*

SCIARRONE
There she is!

SPOLETTA
(Charging toward Tosca)
Ah, Tosca, you will pay for his life most dearly!
*(Tosca springs to her feet, pushing Spoletta
violently, answering:)*

TOSCA
With my own!
*(Spoletta falls back from the sudden thrust.
Tosca escapes and runs to the parapet. She leaps
onto it and hurls herself over the ledge and into the
Tiber River crying:)*

Oh, Scarpia! Before God!
*(Sciarrone and soldiers rush in confusion to
the parapet and look down. Spoletta stands stunned*

*and pale as he sees Tosca's lifeless body being
swept away in the current.)*

"What happened?" Giselle asked frantically as she
rushed to Sarah's side. Stagehands carried her on a stretcher
into the dressing room and hoisted the actress,
semiconscious, to the settee.

"Someone moved the mattress under the parapet
after I checked it," said Adolpho, whose face was beet red
and his brow beaded with sweat. He angrily shooed the
peering cast from Sarah's door and closed it. "Her right
knee landed on the floorboards. We've called for an
ambulance." He wrung his hands in distress.

Giselle pulled up Sarah's dress to her thigh. Her
knee was bleeding and already swelling. She rushed away to
fetch some ice.

Sarah managed to sit up before she returned.

"Take me to the hotel," she said to Giselle as she
applied the ice.

"But madame, you are injured. You need to go to the
hospital! Adolpho has called an ambulance."

"Nonsense!" Sarah said. "Cancel the ambulance!"

When she arrived at Hotel Atlantico, the manager
assisted her to her room and ensured she had everything she
needed for comfort.

"Giselle, please check with the concierge and make
sure we have transportation to the port for our trip home."

"Madame, I know we were planning to leave
tomorrow, but you can hardly walk!"

"Yes, but it is bearable. I just want to get to New
York. Then I will reassess my knee and decide what to do."

"Very well."

The next day, Sarah boarded the ocean liner *Majesto*. By the time she arrived in New York a week later, her leg was so swollen that she had to remain in bed for fifteen days at the Astor House hotel before returning to France.

"Madame, are you sure the world is ready for film?" Giselle asked.

"It's the future!" Sarah thrust her index finger in the air. She briskly walked through her living room in her nightclothes, her purple silk robe flowing behind her. "Besides, I will be one of the first actresses to perform in film. What could be more exciting than that?"

Sarah played Hamlet in the 1900 two-minute film *Le Duel d'Hamlet*. Accompanying the film was a recording of the sword fight. The clashing of the wooden swords hadn't been loud enough, so director Clement Maurice enlisted the aid of a stagehand to bang pieces of metal together in sync with the fight. It was the first sound film.

Sarah's first successful film both in France and in America was *La Dame aux Camelias*, called *Camille*, produced in 1908. She performed opposite her co-star and lover Lou Tellegen. All the while, her injured knee remained painful and swelled upon occasion.

"Are you sure you're healed enough for this? You know how demanding this play can be." Giselle transferred Sarah's clothes from the trunk to the hotel dresser. They were in Berlin, Germany, for a short theater tour.

"I have a commitment. I've signed a contract. I'll be fine." But Sarah knew she wasn't. Her knee was more painful than ever and the swelling now constant.

During rehearsals the next day for *L'Algion, a* Napoleonic play by Edmond Rostand, Sarah experienced excruciating pain in her right knee. She refused to quit but had to limit her stage movements. When she saw a German doctor, he recommended she stop performing and undergo surgery. Recuperation called for six months of immobilizing her leg.

"I won't hear of it!" Sarah told him.

In the summer of 1914, Sarah was on holiday with family and close friends at her vacation home on Belle-Ile, a small island off the coast of Brittany, when she received word of the assassination of Austro-Hungarian Archduke Franz Ferdinand. Due to the political turmoil it aroused throughout Europe, Sarah hurried back to Paris, where she received word that an approaching German army was threatening to invade the city. At the insistence of the minister of war, who wanted to protect the country's most beloved thespian and national treasure, she fled to a villa on the Bay of Arcachon on the southwest coast of France. While there, she saw Dr. Thomas, a physician whom she had visited in Paris. He examined her leg.

"It must be done. The gangrene has infected your leg to the point of being life threatening," he said. "Saving it is pointless. It must come off."

Sarah appreciated his bluntness because she was a get-to-the-point person herself, but the thought of losing her leg was abhorrent. How would she walk? How would she act? She had relied on her leg even while knowing something was terribly wrong. The truth was sobering.

On February 22, 1915, at the age of 71, her right leg was amputated almost to the hip. Dr. Thomas suggested she use an artificial limb.

"I will not wear one!" Sarah said.

"Then you must use crutches or a wheelchair."

"Impossible!" Sarah wanted to hold her head high. She didn't want people to feel sorry for her by relying on artificial means.

"Just how will you get around?" Dr. Thomas thrust his hands on his hips by her bed in exasperation.

Sarah sat up and stretched her neck before looking the doctor squarely in the eye.

"I will design a palanquin on which to be carried. The chair will be decorated in Louis XV style — white sides and gilded trim. It will rest on a platform supported by a pair of long horizontal poles that two men will carry on their shoulders."

The doctor's eyebrows shot up. "And acting? Surely, you'll give that up."

"Never!" She turned her head and stuck her nose in the air.

Sarah relented and tried several wooden legs but threw each away because they were uncomfortable and inhibited her movement. She finally resorted to being carried in a sedan chair, yet, it was far less elaborate than the one she had described to Dr. Thomas.

In October 1915, Sarah returned to the stage. By 1920, she had headlined scores of productions in her theater by rearranging the scenes to accommodate her seated in a chair or supported by a prop that hid her legs.

One night during a dress rehearsal of the play *Un Sujet de Roman* by Sacha Guitry, she collapsed and fell into a coma for an hour. When she awoke she asked, "When do I go on?"

She never did.

Instead, she convalesced for four months and improved enough to continue rehearsals for her new role as Cleopatra. She also prepared to make *La Voyante* a movie by Sasha Guitry. Too weak to travel, however, she reconfigured part of her home as a film studio with scenery, lights, and cameras.

Before she could complete any films in her new home studio, Sarah collapsed again. On March 26, 1923, with her son, Maurice, by her side and wearing the sapphire ring, she died at the age of seventy-nine from renal failure.

~~~

Father Albert included a final handwritten note:

The day of her funeral, over thirty thousand people filed past her casket at the Eglise Saint Francois de Sales to pay their respects. The enormous procession behind her casket proceeded to Cimetiere du Pere-Lachaise and paused for a minute of silence outside her theater to pay homage to the world's most beloved and renowned actress that the papers called "the queen of the pose and the princess of the gesture."

Maurice inherited his mother's possessions, including the sapphire ring. He held onto it for many years in memory of his mother but eventually sold it to a Paris jeweler. He used the money to fund his gambling addiction.

~

Abel closed *Women of the Ring* and put it on the table. He assumed the jeweler who bought the ring from Maurice was the one who sold it to Dolly O'Brien, who in turn gave it to Louise. From Mary of Burgundy to Julia Townsend and now back to France, the ring had traveled full circle. He had concluded the first part of his mission, but the most important part lay ahead.

He walked to the bookshelves and scanned the myriad books. What fascinating stories might they hold? He chose one at random and opened it. The writing was faded, but every page was filled with personal information – names, dates, notes made by the parish priest of the time.

"I see you're through."

Abel jumped as he heard Father Albert's voice behind him. "I was so absorbed in reading these entries I didn't hear you come in."

"After you leave tonight, I will add what you've told me about the ring being purchased by Dolly and presented to Louise, its transfer to her sister, Vera, and then to her niece, Julia's grandmother. Julia's entry will be the last. That will complete the story. Tomorrow night, we'll conclude our mission. It's been arranged."

"I'd better get a good night's sleep then." Abel returned the book to the shelf.

He shook Father Albert's hand and walked back to the hotel midafternoon. The twenty-minute stroll gave him an opportunity to ponder the task ahead. He would be relieved to complete the mission, of course, but he was apprehensive about the consequences. He had a plan to address those and wanted to think it through before he laid his head on the pillow.

Abel's sleep was fitful that night — 1:10 a.m., 2:37 a.m., 4:22 a.m. It wasn't just their mission that kept awakening him. *The consequences, the consequences.* When he flew back to New York, his actions would become most evident. He tried to rationalize them by telling himself that some actions, even those considered morally wrong, are sometimes necessary to achieve morally right outcomes. In his heart of hearts, he knew he had no choice. But would she really understand?

She would have to.

Chapter 18

The next morning at 8:00 a.m., Abel took a long shower in the petite hotel bathroom. He ordered orange juice, a fried egg, and toast from room service and watched a couple of comedies on British cable TV stations. Though his body was tired from the restless night, his mind was alert and on mission.

At one o'clock, he headed to the church. Father Albert had suggested that he enter through the front doors of the sanctuary so he could take in some of its beauty because this would be his last time in the church. He'd never entered that way before.

The church, fronting the street, and the surrounding cemetery extended two long blocks. The architecture was simple, yet elegant, with four tall steeples. The front steps led to ten-foot-tall double wooden doors. Inside the sanctuary, wooden arches supported the expansive dome-shaped ceiling. Intricate stained glass windows and ornate frescos depicting scenes from the Bible covered both sidewalls. Madonna and child, the largest glass window, took up the entire wall behind the pulpit. Wooden pews with red velvet cushions ran the width of the sanctuary from back to front. Five smaller arches along the right side created a hallway with two doors.

After absorbing the sanctuary's splendor, Abel walked through the arched corridor and opened one of the doors. Now he was back to the familiar long hallway he had traversed numerous times during the past three days. It led to the library at the east end of the building, while the west end housed the kitchen along with Father Albert's living quarters, guest room, and office.

Abel couldn't find Father Albert in the library, so he headed toward the kitchen. Perhaps the priest had fixed a late lunch? He wasn't there either, and all seemed quiet.

Too quiet.

Abel's eyes stopped on a wooden chair on the far side of the table. It had been knocked to the floor. As he bent over to right the chair, his breath caught in his throat. Father Albert was sprawled face down on the floor behind the table, his arm hiding his face. Abel knelt beside the priest and turned him over. He gasped when he saw Father Albert's face – scraped and bloody, his bottom lip split and bruised. Lacerations on his cheeks were bleeding too.

Abel was about to summon help when Father Albert opened his eyes.

"What happened?" Abel asked.

"Masego," Father Albert said through blood-stained teeth. "I had just gotten it out of the safe when he came in.

He demanded I give it to him. When I refused . . . well . . . you can see. I made it to the kitchen, but that's as far as I got."

"Don't move, I'm going for help!" Abel's gaze located the wall phone next to the door.

Father Albert tried to get up and grabbed Abel's arm. "There's no time. You must go after him!"

"I can't leave you here."

Father Albert's grip tightened. "He's got the ring!"

Adrenalin surged through Abel. "I'll find him."

On his way out, Abel ran into one of the nuns and told her about Father Albert. Then he rushed down the street to the jewelry store as though the adrenalin spike had cured his limp, though he still clutched his cane. Celeste greeted him from behind the counter when he entered.

"Mr. Moody, how nice to see you again." She gave him a broad smile.

"Masego." Abel's hard stare reinforced his intent.

"He . . . he's not here." Celeste said, taken aback.

Abel took a deep breath.

"I'm sorry to be so abrupt, Celeste, but it's very important that I find him. Where did he go?" Abel's hand gripped his cane as though he could reduce it to sawdust.

"He rushed in, then out. Said he had to go to the bank."

Right, to put the ring into a safety deposit box, Abel surmised. The mission he had come all this way for would be thwarted if he didn't find Masego before he reached the bank. He couldn't let that happen.

"Which bank?"

"Banque Barclays. Down the street a couple of blocks." Celeste pointed to the right. "What's this all about, monsieur?"

Abel hurried out the door instead of answering.

The Paris sidewalks bristled with locals and tourists brave enough to endure the chill of forty-one degrees and overcast skies. How would he ever find Masego before he reached the bank? He still had to try despite Masego's head start.

Able's eyes darted from one pedestrian to the next, and his mind eliminated the women in scarfs and hats and concentrated on the men. How tall was Masego? About his own height, he remembered. What kind and color of coat had he worn to the café? A long dark-gray one. No hat.

Abel scanned the backs of the men. With the crowd, however, all he could see was from their waists up. Not much to go on. What about his head, his hair? He was black — maybe look for dark skin. But with collars pulled up around the men's necks to ward off the cold, all he could see was the back of their heads. Not much help. Still, Abel pressed on.

He approached the first intersection and noticed a man up ahead that might fit the description. If only he could get closer. Fortunately, the stoplight was delaying the man on the curb. In a few seconds, he'd be just behind him.

As Abel closed in about fifteen feet from the man, the light changed and the crowd moved in a wave across the street. Abel merged with them, his eyes glued to the man's back. As they passed a couple of stores, the man raised his cell phone to his ear. While talking into it, he hesitated before glancing back as if looking for someone. His eyes locked onto Abel.

Masego.

Had Carmen called to warn him?

Masego quickened his pace. So did Abel.

Masego stopped in the middle of the block and looked across the street. Abel followed his gaze . . . Banque Barclays!

Masego looked back at Abel, back at the bank, then again at Abel, as though calculating whether he could cross the street. The traffic was thick, though, with cars, taxis, and delivery trucks zooming past. Masego couldn't cross without being hit. He'd have to cross at the next intersection.

Masego marched on. Abel followed. Without warning, Masego stepped off the curb.

A horn blared. Tires screeched. A loud thud. Screams.

By the time Abel got to Masego, blood was beginning to pool around his head in the gutter. His crumpled body resembled a rag doll tossed into a closet. The deliveryman who hit him was hovering over Masego with a distraught expression, his damaged van behind him. Some people were trying to stop the bleeding. Others were calling the police on their cell phones.

Abel knelt beside Masego and nonchalantly tried to feel his coat pockets for the ring box. Nothing. Then he spotted a dirty, crushed white box lying in the gutter. Had the accident jarred it from Masego's coat pocket? Abel inconspicuously wrapped his long fingers around the box and snuck it into his right pants pocket. Then noting that Masego was being attended to by several in the crowd, he casually stepped back onto the curb and blended into the gathering throng.

"It was awful." Abel sat in a chair, elbows on his knees and head in his palms, beside Father Albert's hospital bed.

"I'm sure it was." Father Albert slurred his words, trying not to aggravate his swollen, bruised lip. His head was wrapped in bandages, and an IV snaked up his arm. His left cheek was swollen where the lacerations had been stitched.

"He'd still be alive if I hadn't been following him."

"If Masego hadn't assaulted me and stolen the ring, you wouldn't have been following him. You can't blame yourself for this tragedy. You didn't push him into the traffic."

"I realize that, but it doesn't erase what I saw or feel."

"Perhaps it wasn't an accident."

Abel's head jerked up. "What do you mean?"

"Is it possible Masego stepped off of the curb on purpose? Assault and larceny are considered felonies. His penalty would have been quite severe, his prison term long. Besides, the public doesn't look kindly on people who assault priests. His reputation would have been irreparably damaged as well as his business. Maybe he didn't want to face the consequences. Maybe this was his way out."

"I never even considered that, but it could make sense. He did hesitate once at the curb as though trying to decide what to do."

"Well, I will pray for your peace and for Masego's soul."

"Thank you, Father."

"You realize I won't be able to go with you this evening?"

"Of course, I understand."

"You don't mind going alone?"

"Not at all. It has to be done, especially in light of what just happened. Perhaps the so-called curse extends beyond the women of the ring."

"Perhaps, but I'd like to see the ring one last time before you go. You do have it?"

"Wouldn't let it out of my possession now." Abel withdrew the battered box from his pants pocket and handed it to Father Albert.

The priest removed the lid and held the ring up to toward the western window. The gems sparkled in the fading afternoon sun as he angled it to see it more clearly.

"It really is quite beautiful," he said.

"No question about that."

"And such a history. The images of the falcon between the smaller gems take me back to the first story of Mary of Burgundy. Such a tragic ending."

Abel nodded.

Father Albert tucked the ring back into the box and handed it to Abel.

"Very well, then. Here is the information you'll need." Father Albert handed Abel a piece of paper with a name, address, and phone number. "I will phone ahead and let them know you are coming alone. Go with God's blessing." He made the sign of the cross.

Chapter 19

Julia pressed the buzzer at the front door of Moody's Jewelry & Repair for the third time.

"I don't understand why he isn't answering. He said for us to be here at three o'clock sharp when I met him downtown for lunch on Tuesday after his visit with his lawyer and financial advisor. What time do you have?" She looked at Winston, who had come with her to retrieve their engagement ring. They had been back in Brooklyn about five days.

Winston pulled his phone from his jacket pocket and squinted at the display in the sunlight. "I have 3:05. Let's give him another couple of minutes." Winston pocketed his phone and rubbed his hands together for warmth.

Julia took a deep breath and peered through the door. "Maybe he's up in his apartment. He wouldn't hear the buzzer." She stepped back and looked up toward the second floor. Winston stepped back and looked up toward the windows as well.

"See him?" Julia asked.

"The curtains are open, but I don't see him. I guess we can always come back."

"Mr. Moody was very emphatic that we meet him here at this time. He said everything was ready to be picked up. When I asked him what 'everything' was, he said he had a gift for us for our engagement. I just can't believe he'd tell us to come by the store and then not show up. It certainly isn't like him. Maybe something happened."

Winston rolled his eyes. "Are we going to go through that again?"

Julia scowled at Winston. They waited another ten minutes, intermittently phoning him on his cell, store, and apartment phones and pressing the buzzer. Each of Mr. Moody's phones went to voice mail, and he never came to the door. Winston headed for the car.

"Wait," Julia said. "I just remembered he has a doorbell to his apartment at the rear entrance. I'm going around back." She headed down the sidewalk and around the building.

"Why didn't we try that the last time?" Winston followed close behind.

"It's been a long time, Winston. I didn't remember it then. Besides, his store was locked up tight, the security gate down, and a note that he'd left on an emergency. This time the store's open, but he isn't answering."

The alley was remarkably devoid of clutter and litter with only a few garbage cans and empty old wooden crates sitting outside a row of doors. Julia stopped at a red door, rang the doorbell and waited. No answer.

"We'll just have to come back," Winston said.

"But we need the ring for the engagement party tomorrow night, and the store is closed on Sundays."

"Well, what's your suggestion?"

Julia thought for a moment. Then she grabbed Winston's arm. "Oh my gosh, Winston! I just remembered something Mr. Moody asked me at lunch. I thought it odd at the time, but now it makes sense."

"What did he ask you?"

"If I remembered where he kept the door key. When I was a teen visiting Mr. Moody and his wife, he showed me where they kept the extra key. I think he wants us to go in."

Winston stood hands on hips as Julia felt behind the carriage light fixture next to the door. Eureka! She pulled out a key and waggled it at Winston. She took a deep breath, slid it into the lock and twisted. The dead bolt released with a click.

"Are you coming?" Julia looked over her shoulder at Winston.

"You know I'm not in favor of this."

"Yes, I know, but I really feel like something has happened to Mr. Moody. We have to check and make sure he's okay."

Julia turned the doorknob and entered. To her right were the stairs that led to Mr. Moody's apartment. In front of her was the back door to the store.

"Look, Winston." Julia pointed at the display on the alarm next to the back door. "The security system has been turned off. That means Mr. Moody was in the store. Let's look there first."

Julia pushed open the door and called Mr. Moody's name. No answer once again. She and Winston entered the store, where nothing seemed disturbed. They searched the back room with Mr. Moody's desk. Julia noticed a stack of papers on top and thumbed through them.

"Well, he's been here. There are signed receipts for orders that were picked up earlier today." She flashed one of them at Winston. "Look at this one. It says the customer picked up a necklace at 1:30. If he was here then, why isn't he here now?" Julia returned the receipt to the stack. "We need to check the apartment."

Winston followed Julia as they retraced their steps out the back door to the bottom of the apartment stairs.

"I'll go first." Winston started up the steps. "Mr. Moody? Mr. Moody? It's Winston and Julia." His voice echoed off the wood walls of the narrow stairwell as they gingerly ascended. At the landing, they looked at each other wide eyed. The door was ajar.

With Winston's head above Julia's, they peered through the narrow opening into the living room. Light from the windows illuminated a package wrapped in blue paper and tied with a large white bow on the dining room table. A smaller white box sat on top.

"It must be our engagement our ring!" Julia said. "And look, Winston, underneath is our engagement present."

"Mr. Moody? Are you there?" Winston called through the opening.

Still no answer.

"We have to go in." Julia pushed on the door.

She and Winston went directly to the table to examine what Mr. Moody had left for them. Along with the gifts were two envelopes – a large manila envelope and a smaller white one.

"It says 'Open This First.'" Winston held up the manila envelope addressed to Julia.

"See? I knew he meant for us to come in."

"I see you found everything."

Julia jumped. She brought her hand to her chest as she turned toward the voice. She let out a big sigh of relief.

"Oh, Mr. Moody, you scared me! Are you okay? Winston and I were so worried when you didn't answer." She gave Mr. Moody a hug. He returned it.

"I'm fine, Miss Julia. No need to worry. I was in the bathroom and didn't hear you." Mr. Moody stood in his bedroom doorway.

Julia's brow creased in concern as her eyes rested on the suitcase by his side. "Are you going someplace?"

"Back to Paris."

"Paris! Why?"

"It's time for me to go, Miss Julia."

"Go? But, I don't understand, Mr. Moody. You've been like a father to me. I was so hoping you'd be at the engagement party tomorrow." Tears brimmed in Julia's eyes and tumbled down her cheeks.

Mr. Moody pulled a handkerchief from his pocket and handed it to her. "Miss Julia, it's hard to explain. I can only hope you'll understand when you open your gifts."

Just then a horn honked twice.

"It's my taxi. I've got to go. Just know that I love you, Miss Julia." Mr. Moody gave Julia a long hug, then grabbed his suitcase.

"I love you too," Julia said. A bewildered expression covered her face as she watched Mr. Moody descend the stairs.

Winston moved to Julia's side and pulled her close. "I think he wants you to open the envelope." He handed it to her.

She withdrew several legal documents. "What in the world in this?"

Clipped on top was a three-page letter in Mr. Moody's handwriting addressed to Julia. She furrowed her brow as she read it. Halfway through, her chin quivered and tears tumbled onto the letter. After reading it, she handed it to Winston and scanned the documents.

She brushed away her tears and slipped the documents back into the manila envelope. Inside the smaller envelope was a card congratulating her and Winston on their engagement and letting them know the large box contained their engagement present. The smaller box held their ring. She handed the card to Winston and reached for the small white box.

She hesitated and inhaled deeply before lifting the lid.

Chapter 20
Six months later

Julia leaned against the front door frame of Moody's Jewelry & Repair and gazed toward the street. A young girl about ten stopped and looked in the store widow, her nose so close to the glass that she left the imprint of her breath on it. She was dressed in blue shorts and a yellow T-shirt, both unkempt.

"Hi, my name's Julia. Do you like jewelry?"

The girl's eyes never wavered from the window. "Oh, I love jewelry, especially rings." She held up her hands to display every finger adorned with a cheap ring. Some with colored glass looked like they came from a gumball machine or flea market.

"Would you like to come in and see our rings up close?"

"I could never afford any of these."

"Well, it doesn't cost anything to look, right?"

The girl turned and caught Julia with her dark brown eyes. "This your store?"

"It is now. I inherited it from Mr. Moody, a very good friend of mine. He used to own it."

"What happened to him? He die?"

Julia let out a muffled laugh. "No, he's still alive. He moved to Paris and is living it up in his old age with a good friend of his named Father Albert."

"So he just gave you his store and all the jewelry?"

"Not exactly. It was in exchange for a family heirloom that was very precious to me."

"What was that?"

"It's a long story, but it involves something you'd be very interested in — a ring."

"Whoa, he gave you this whole store for a ring?" The white around the girl's dark irises expanded in amazement.

"Yes, would you like to see it?"

The girl looked at the window and back at Julia. "Would I!"

"By the way, what's your name?"

"Alisha." She pointed at the contemporary gold ring with two large diamonds on Julia's left hand. "Did Mr. Moody make that?"

"Yes, it's my engagement ring." Julia raised her hand so Alisha could inspect the ring.

"Wow, it's beautiful!" Alisha said. "When's the wedding?"

"Next month," Julia said with a smile.

Alisha moved into the store. "You make all this jewelry?"

"No, no, I'm not the jeweler. Carl, a very skilled artisan, makes the jewelry. He lives upstairs above the shop. He's not here just now."

Julia watched Alisha walk the length of the glass counters while gawking at all the fine jewelry. It reminded Julia of herself when she had been so mesmerized by all the glittering pieces in Mr. Moody's shop the very first time.

"So which one of these rings was yours?" Alisha pointed at the display of gold and silver rings set with sparkling diamonds and gems.

"Actually, that ring isn't in any of the cases. It's there." Julia pointed at a large framed photo of the sapphire ring on the wall. It was the only photo she had of the ring, the one she had shown her grandmother.

"So it's not real, just a photo?" Alisha's brow crinkled as though she'd been deceived.

"Oh, it's very real, but it's not here."

Alisha cocked her head. "Then where is it?"

"In Belgium. Ever heard of that country?"

"Not really," Alisha said.

"Well, Belgium is in Europe, just to the north of France and across the English channel from England."

Alisha shrugged as though England and France were foreign to her. "So where in Belgium is the ring?"

"It's in a very special place — the tomb of Mary of Burgundy in the Church of Our Lady. Mr. Moody put it there."

"Why would anyone put such a beautiful ring in a grave?" Alisha scrunched her face in disgust.

"He did it out of love, to protect me, and he felt it should be laid to rest with the woman it was designed to honor."

"What did you need protecting from, some gang or Mafia person?"

Julia chuckled. "No, nothing like that, but some people thought the ring was cursed."

"Cursed? Like voodoo?" Alisha shrunk back.

"Well, some people felt that whoever owned the ring had really bad luck. Mr. Moody didn't want anything bad to happen to me, so he put the ring in the coffin."

Alisha turned back to the photo. "What are those little marks between the smaller stones?"

"They're birds — falcons to be specific."

"Huh, they don't look like birds."

"Here, let me show you something." Julia ducked into the back room and emerged with a book about the size of an accounting ledger. It was bound in dark leather and embossed with the falcon image on the front.

"What's that?" Alisha pointed at the book.

"This is the story of the ring. Would you like to read it?"

Alisha cocked her head and hesitated. Then she nodded.

Julia pulled two chairs close together and beckoned Alisha to sit with her. They balanced the book on their laps, and Julia opened it to the title page: *Women of the Ring.*

ABOUT THE AUTHOR

Sally J. Ling, Florida's History Detective, is an author, speaker, and historian. She writes historical nonfiction, specializing in obscure, unusual, or little known stories of Florida history, as well as historical fiction and biblical mysteries with a Florida connection.

As a special correspondent, Sally wrote for the *Sun Sentinel* newspaper for four years and was a contributing journalist for several South Florida magazines.

Based upon her knowledge as well as excerpts from her books, Sally has appeared in three feature-length TV documentaries—"Gangsters," the National Geographic Channel; "Boca Raton: The Secret Weapon that Won World War II" and "Prohibition and the South Florida Connection," WLRN, Miami. She served as associate producer on the latter production. She has also appeared in and served as production consultant for several short documentaries on South Florida history produced by WLRN, Miami.

Sally has been a repeat guest on South Florida PBS TV and radio stations, guest presenter at the Lifelong Learning Society at Florida Atlantic University and Future Authors of America, and guest speaker at numerous historical societies, libraries, organizations, and schools.

Sally lives with her husband, Chuck, and splits her time between South Florida and western North Carolina.

Sally's books include:

Fiction

- *Women of the Ring*
- *Who Killed Leno and Louise?*
- *The Twelfth Stone: A Shea Baker Mystery (Volume 3)*
- *The Spear of Destiny: A Shea Baker Mystery (Volume 2)*
- *The Cloak: A Shea Baker Mystery (Volume 1)*
- *The Tree and the Carpenter*
- *Spies, Root Beer and Alligators: Phillip's Great Adventures (Children's Novel)*

Nonfiction

- *Al Capone's Miami: Paradise or Purgatory?*
- *Out of Mind, Out of Sight: A Revealing History of the Florida State Hospital at Chattahoochee and Mental Health Care in Florida*
- *Sailin' on the Stranahan* (commissioned coffee table book)

- *Run the Rum In: South Florida during Prohibition*
- *Small Town, Big Secrets: Inside the Boca Raton Army Airfield during World War II (First and Second editions)*
- *A History of Boca Raton*
- *Fund Raising With Golf*

For information on Sally's current projects, or to become a "Preferred Reader," please visit her website at: _sallyjling.com._

To engage Sally as a speaker, or to send her an email, contact her at:
info@sallyjling.com

www.ingramcontent.com/pod-product-compliance
Lightning Source LLC
Chambersburg PA
CBHW071150170626
46809CB00002B/841